THE UNLIKELY REDEMPTION OF THE THIEF SYDNEY BRIDGEWATER

A NOVEL BY

MIC LOWTHER

Olympus Story House

TABLE OF CONTENTS

Part One: Squaring Up

CHAPTER 1

Avoiding Attention

Sydney Bridgewater – born in the South, always lived in the South, enjoyed being warm in the South – had now endured four North Dakota winters.

Winters were miserable in North Dakota. The only reason she hadn't fled back to Oklahoma during her first year of below-zero temperatures was that she'd found opportunities for personal profit in the oil fields to be as endless as the snow- and wind-swept prairie outside her office window.

The computer analyst job she'd found had captured her interest, and the people she worked with – who'd been there many more winters than four – had proved competent and pleasant.

And the surrounding territory had been more interesting to explore in spring, summer, and fall than she'd first thought. She'd visited Garrison Dam, driven the Enchanted Highway, seen the world's largest buffalo statue, gone to zoos, museums, national parks, historical sights, natural wonders, centers for various cultural heritages, and learned more about Lewis and Clark than she'd ever thought she'd find interesting.

But four winters were enough. As the weather began turning cold again, she bid farewell to Tioga (North Dakota's oil capital), returned to Oklahoma City, moved into a two-bedroom apartment, and turned the thermostat to 80°.

For those who haven't met the thief, Sydney Bridgewater, now 48 years old, the sources of her current bank balance of $21 million were computer modules she'd painstakingly written and embedded in the computers of five previous employers, including the one she'd just departed. Each coding masterwork skimmed a small, relatively insignificant dollar amount off transactions being processed and sent it along a devious and complicated path to Sydney's personal bank account. This had been going on since she was 20, a few thousand per month from each place she'd worked, and it had added up.

Her code was protected. If any of it were deleted or corrupted somehow, a dedicated OverWatch component would automatically reinstall it. If a nosy programmer somewhere started snooping through it, OverWatch would alert her. If she wanted to revise skimming parameters up or down, OverWatch enabled her to do so remotely.

And should it become necessary to delete her code permanently for some catastrophic reason, she could also do that remotely. She'd aptly named that last-ditch measure DefCon2.

Protection didn't end there. She had 53 bank accounts across the USA opened under various names. The $21 million was deposited more or less evenly in five of them. Every eight days, a routine on her computer transferred these deposits, plus new money received, to five different accounts it chose randomly from the 53.

If someone did discover one of her many accounts, nine chances out of ten on any given day, there would be nothing in it. And the seemingly high transfer activity wouldn't be noticeable because any one account would only be used, on average, about four times a year. Her money – and she did consider it hers – was safe and had been year after year.

Yet now Sydney grew concerned. She'd received three intrusion alarms recently and her code had been deleted (but automatically reinstalled) at one site. There'd been no follow-up activity, no increased flurry of intrusions, but she was suspicious. Someone might be sniffing around, and she didn't like it. Was it accidental, or was someone on her trail? Had the risk of what she was doing gone up?

The prospect of discovery, present in the background all these years, was chilling. She didn't want to be talked about, dissected, humiliated, and dragged through the mud by the press. She might be overreacting – very likely was – but wasn't one to ignore potential threats.

She called an attorney for an appointment.

Wearing a lavender sheath dress falling well short of her knees, Sydney stood on the sidewalk in front of the Skirvin Hilton Hotel at One Park Avenue in downtown Oklahoma City at three o'clock on a Tuesday afternoon. She sported a wide-brimmed straw hat with a lavender band; large, square-framed tortoiseshell sunglasses; carried an oversized black leather shoulder bag with lavender accents; wore sheer black stockings with perfectly straight seams; and stood motionless in strappy lavender evening sandals with five-inch stiletto heels.

She'd been waiting there three minutes.

Passers-by – pedestrians and those in vehicles alike – noticed her, slowed, and turned to look back when they'd passed.

She gave no sign of recognition.

Then a limo bearing the inscription "Nowhere to go but everywhere" drew up to the curb. The driver, dressed in proper chauffeur attire, got out and opened the rear door. Sydney got in without a word. The driver returned to his seat and the limo pulled away, going on to deliver her two minutes later to a tall building that dominated the downtown skyline. She paid him $200.

Quentin Underwood, a black man with a Morgan Freeman complexion, known in the community as Quentin the Quintessential, noticed her arrival in his waiting room.

"Ms. Bridgewater," he said.

"I am," Sydney replied.

He welcomed her into his office, saying, "Please forgive me for commenting, but you are stunningly overdressed for the occasion."

"Intentionally so," Sydney replied. "I didn't want to be recognized."

"How so?"

"This outfit has many distracting elements: short skirt, square sunglasses, wide-brimmed hat, black seamed stockings, and stiletto evening sandals in mid-afternoon. A casual passerby's glance would be too busy to settle on my face. In case anyone was following me, it was a way of avoiding attention by attracting attention."

"Brilliant, so how may I help you?"

"I have several bank accounts throughout the US which add up to a bit over $21 million," she said without preamble. "I wish to open an account at Dreyfus Bank in Switzerland and move most of this money there."

"You can do that independently; you don't need my help."

"I believe I do," Sydney said. "Protection and secrecy laws would no longer apply if Dreyfus or any other institution were presented with evidence my funds were illegally obtained. The bank could give investigating authorities access to my information and allow them to freeze or even confiscate the entire amount."

"*Was* the money obtained illegally?" Quentin asked.

"Yes, I stole all of it," Sydney replied confidently, "a little at a time, very quietly and patiently over 28 years."

"And no one found out?"

"No."

"Though I'm certainly curious about how you managed this," the attorney said, "I do not need to know just now. But I must know one thing: is it still going on?"

"Yes, it is."

Quentin the Quintessential sat in silence for a long while. He looked up a couple of things on his computer, then sat in silence a bit more.

Sydney waited.

"There are several issues at play here," Quentin finally said. "First, I cannot represent you if you are still involved in illegal activity. It would be my lawyerly duty to inform authorities of an ongoing crime. Before I do any actual work, I want your assurance that whatever you've been doing has ended. Is that a possibility?"

"Yes."

"There is next the matter of limitations. Stealing that much money is a Class B felony and can be prosecuted for up to seven years. You say you did this over 28 years, but I'm speculating you do not have each year's amount isolated in a separate account."

"I do not," Sydney said.

"Then, according to the concept of *commingled funds* – everything mixed together – the entire amount would be treated as if it had been stolen today."

"I see."

"This leaves you two choices: put it all in one place and don't touch it for seven years, or take some proactive move toward making things right. The latter would be the preferred approach but could be risky regarding restitution, possible jail time, pesky news publicity, a felony police record, etc."

"I'm fairly sure I wish to, as you say, make things right," Sydney said. "Would you represent me?"

"What do you hope to accomplish?"

"No prosecution, nothing on my record, and I retain some or all of the money."

"Ambitious, to say the least," Quentin said, "but perhaps possible. I would require a $500,000 retainer to get started."

"Agreed," Sydney said without hesitation.

"Then you have a bit of work to do. Let me know when you can proceed, and we'll talk further."

She rose, thanked the attorney, and left the office.

But she did not immediately leave the building. She carried the shoulder bag into the restroom and, a few minutes later emerged wearing a Newsboy cap, cheap sunglasses, denim jacket and jeans, and yellow Converse high-tops. Lavender Lady was now in her bag. She walked to a waiting taxi, which took her to her car at the Skirvin Hilton, and then drove home.

The attorney's requirement to shut down her skimming operation was what she'd expected. Incidents of snooping into her code had been initial nudges to do something.

This drastic move was that "something."

CHAPTER 2

Hire You Back in An Instant

On an inconsequential day of an insignificant month in an unremarkable dead of night, Sydney Bridgewater initiated DefCon2 with three seconds of clicking on her keyboard.

There was no "Are you sure?"

At lightspeed, her command traveled to five computers in five different cities, and her long-secret program code vanished, never to be found, never to return.

As risky as it may turn out to be, she'd decided, it was time to move on.

"It's done," she reported to her attorney the next day. She handed him a check for the requested retainer, a list of companies affected, and a roughly estimated amount stolen from each.

"Excellent," Quentin responded. "I'll begin by scheduling meetings, then traveling to each location to negotiate with the company attorney. You should allow about three months for me to reach some conclusion, whatever it may turn out to be. I'll keep you informed."

But three months was a long time to wait. Sydney liked to keep busy, to have some project with a definable product at its conclusion. It didn't take her long to come up with one.

Computer virus programs – those that protected computers against unwelcome intruders – were defensive in design. Their mission was to protect.

What if they *attacked* instead of merely defending against the intruder?

Preliminary designs began appearing in her mind. A hacker got in but left a trail she could follow back out. Once inside the hacker's computer, she could interrupt or even take over its functions. She could be polite and show a stern warning message, or she could go all Genghis Khan and trash the computer completely. It would take only seconds.

She got to work.

She had a preliminary model within a month. She tested with two of her computers, one hacking in and the other fighting back. This led to refinements giving both more capabilities.

She was ready to test online by the end of the second month. She prepared a program with five levels of security, each more demanding than the last, each with a corresponding and more severe attack profile. She offered prizes for reaching each level and invited the hacker community to do its best. She also issued a strict warning: Back up your computer before beginning; it *will* be destroyed.

Intruders appeared at once. Most got past level one security; fewer got by level two. Sydney's code issued warnings at each level and disabled something on the invading computer. Only a few survived level three; by the time they entered level four, their computer had been rendered inoperable. By the end of the week, no one had made it any further.

Sydney paid out prize money, made a few program changes, then restarted the challenge with increased prize amounts. She did the same during the third and fourth weeks. Still, no one survived past level four.

She received more than a hundred messages reporting computers being left totally unusable. She also received threats of legal action against her, along with several inquiries about purchasing her program. She figured offers for absurdly high amounts were from companies wanting to shelve the program so it never saw the light of day, but others were worth considering. She would surely sell it; developing an ongoing sales and maintenance operation was beyond her interest.

Which is when she received a call from Quentin the Quintessential.

"I met with attorneys for all five of your former employers," he said, "and the meetings were most curious. Each proceeded along the same basic path: 1) disbelief that any such theft had occurred, 2) a subsequent period in which the company analyzed their financial records, 3) concluding opinions saying that though they'd found scattered irregularities, there was no substantiation of large amounts of money missing, and 4) a proposed contingency settlement should there be anything to settle.

"I must say I am truly impressed," Quentin said. "You stole $21 million, or so you say, yet no one seems to know anything about it. Nor do they care. You covered your tracks well."

"They probably looked for large discrepancies, not small ones," Sydney replied.

"Possibly so. In any case, I can report that they would all hire you instantly. Should you need a job, there's an opportunity.

"Next, and here's the excellent news: they prefer you not return the money. It would be awkward to account for, explain to tax accountants and IRS auditors, and be more trouble than it was worth. If nobody has noticed it missing for up to 28 years, more than one said, nobody cares about it now. I must inform you that I encouraged them toward this conclusion.

"Most importantly, they are pleased you came to them first. There was no prominent news story about clandestine thievery to embarrass them and damage their credibility. Having however much money stolen right under their noses would not tell of good stewardship. Instead, your straightforward approach allowed them to sidestep any associated fallout.

"They easily agreed not to press charges and gave me signed documents saying so. But, to respond to your desire to make things right, and in return for letting you off the hook so easily – if indeed you were even *on* a hook for anything – they want you to make some symbolic, substantive effort toward recompense. They're offering you full freedom of ideas here, so what do you suppose that would be?"

"Here's something I've thought about," Sydney replied, "I'll create a million-dollar Internet treasure hunt. Anyone with computer skills and imagination can try his or her hand at digging through a host of clues and obscure literary and cultural references in a quest to discover, somewhere in the vastness of cyberspace, a photo of a small scrap of paper with *You win a million dollars: love, Sydney* written on it. I'll pay the prize money, and the employers will be sponsors. They'll receive free advertising for as long as the hunt continues."

"I think that's an excellent solution," Quentin said. As it turned out, so did all those involved.

Sydney spent a month developing her treasure hunt. It started simply as a game to find something, increased in difficulty by shifting sets of clues and ambiguous references, and then became a labyrinth of words and artifacts that changed their significance and location randomly. She tested it thoroughly then launched it for public use. She deposited $1 million in Quentin the Quintessential's Trust Account for eventual payment to the winner and asked him to notify her former employers of the agreement's completion.

They filed no charges.

The court system never got involved. Sydney Bridgewater was vindicated entirely, and her name never appeared in any official ruling or news broadcast.

She traveled to Switzerland, opened an account at Dreyfus Bank and transferred $20 million to it. "Don't lose it" was the only direction she gave the managing broker.

She sold her hack-attack program for $2 million and hoped to see the result of its expanding use. The playing field would slowly be leveled as hackers suffered the wrath of the program's various levels of devastation.

Then she closed 50 of her 53 bank accounts and distributed her retained onshore balance to the remaining three.

That done, she was officially and certifiably legitimate and had pledged to remain so. She would move on to some new project or life activity that clung more closely to the law.

CHAPTER 3

Some Sort of Crossroad

Sydney Bridgewater sat in her Oklahoma City apartment and contemplated her new state in life.

She was no longer concerned about "someone on her trail." Check.

She'd squared matters with the law and her former employers. Check.

She had a ton of money securely put away and plenty more besides. Check.

It was some sort of crossroad, to be sure, yet she felt no evidence of any magical new virtue. No one looked at her differently or gave her a free ham sandwich. No one applauded her for breaking free of the dark side to embrace the straight and narrow. No one indicated she was now somehow newly enlightened.

She was still just Sydney whom no one knew very well or at all – a status of her own doing. For 28 years she'd reclusively kept to herself, quietly and expertly did whatever job she'd agreed to do, and accumulated money for some eventual purpose she'd never defined.

It was time to "move forward," something told her.

So? Where was forward?

If she was moving on, where was that?

Did she need time to think? Time to evaluate? Time, as popular psychobabble said, "to process?" Maybe, or then again, maybe not.

Her churning thoughts eventually slowed and one thing became clear.

She was whining.

Boo-hoo.

She should *do* something.

Okay then, but even though her bank account would keep her afloat for several lifetimes of *doing nothing*, she needed to work at something and be productive. Watching sunsets in Tahiti, sipping martinis in early afternoon, and touring the world indulgently might be cultured and upper-crusty things to do, but they didn't add up to much of anything. She needed to be busy, not just at a job, but a business. She could afford to fail a time or two; why not start her own?

But her thinking didn't stop there. Pushing on through half an hour of total silence, she devised a plan to earn this new life status Quentin the Quintessential had made possible. It had three steps: she should do something significant: 1) for herself, 2) for a friend, and 3) for someone not her friend.

Since starting a to-do list with something already done was always good, she checked off Step 1. What she had in mind for the remaining two would require an office. Not a tiny office but something bordering on huge. Thus, Sydney fired up her ancient Prius and went shopping.

She cruised business parks on the outskirts of town, then downtown, and got tours from eager leasing agents. She looked at dark, grainy wood offices with nothing but a desk and a chair, suitable perhaps for Sam Spade, and sickly pale green offices with room for 300 stockbrokers yelling into phones. She considered renovating a run-down building adorned with graffiti inside and out and derelicts sleeping in the hallways, or maybe spending a fortune for lavish premium space in a high-rise with uniformed front-door security.

After several days of searching, and in a sudden burst of thinking big, she rented an entire 12,000 foot^2, stand-alone building in a fashionable office park. It had four unfurnished executive offices on the second floor, two more on the first, a large conference room, a modest reception area, and a break room with many cupboards. It was far more space than she needed, but that was today; who knew what she might need tomorrow?

But she did know, and the space was perfect. Besides, the building had been idle for over a year and was a bargain at $22,500 monthly.

She chose a 1,500 foot^2 office upstairs, arranged to have it furnished, and then called in a computer squad. She wanted power, she told them, lots of it.

A week later, she had three of the fastest computers available, a floor-to-ceiling rack of massive disk storage, two color printers, and nine 36-inch computer monitors mounted on a wall in a three-by-three grid. She could view separate images on each screen or spread one image across any adjacent four or all nine.

She displayed the status of her $1 million Internet treasure hunt, going a month now with no winner. No one had gotten even close. Based on what she could see in the display, it would be going on for a long time. But watching it wouldn't offer much diversion; she needed something new and real to do.

She was skilled at using the computer to find things, search out background on things, and use that information to work out a theory and corresponding plan. She could build a business on those skills but needed proper credentials.

So, she went to Private Investigator School. By training as a PI, she could fully understand and do the work and offer more than just friendly advice. She'd be authorized to take action.

Licensing required 55 hours of classwork. She provided background personal and professional information along with fingerprints. She showed proof of citizenship and obtained liability insurance. And, with a silent thanks to Quentin the Quintessential, verified she had no arrest history. Completing this all in three weeks, she passed the final examination and obtained her certification. Then she created a company – Bridgewater Investigations – and began to advertise.

Her company start-up was rough going at first; the phone didn't ring for five days. When it finally did at 2 AM, it was ringing because no one else in town would answer.

Someone's grandfather was missing.

"I'll find him," she confidently told the caller.

She phoned the police. No older adult had been brought to the station.

She phoned a nearby homeless shelter. No such person had come in.

She phoned the bus company. Yes, there was an elderly passenger currently riding a bus that served that neighborhood.

The story soon came together. Grandpa had gotten up in the middle of the night to go to the refrigerator. He took a wrong turn somewhere and ended up in the front yard in his bathrobe and slippers. He wandered out to the sidewalk, then up to the street corner where a city bus had stopped. The bus door looked like the refrigerator, but he didn't remember the refrigerator having stairs. He didn't need bus fare because of his age, so the driver welcomed him aboard and waved him to a seat. He was the only passenger on the bus.

The bus dispatcher told Sydney that if he stayed there, the bus would pass the corner where he'd boarded in about 35 minutes. Sydney called the home number she'd been given and told them to wait at the bus stop. Grandpa would be there soon.

"No charge," Sydney said when asked. "It's this month's start-up special."

Wasn't that fun, Sydney thought, and she'd never even gotten out of bed.

Two days later came another call, this time in mid-afternoon.

"I know my husband is cheating on me," the nervous woman said. "I want you to follow him and find out who she is." Sydney knew from school that this was one of the more frequent PI requests.

"What makes you think so?" she asked.

"Every few nights, he leaves the house just after midnight and he's gone for several hours. I know he's meeting someone."

"Have you asked him about it?"

"No, I'm afraid to."

Sydney agreed and got the particulars she would need. Toward midnight, she drove to the location she'd been given, parked, and waited. Several hours later, she saw him leave his garage. She followed discretely at a distance. He drove leisurely across town and eventually parked at the Metro Technology Center. He walked to the entry door carrying a briefcase and a large block of metal, possibly aluminum. Someone inside let him in.

Sydney waited. Two hours later he emerged alone carrying the same briefcase, but the metal block had been cut and machined into smaller parts, which he carried in a bag. He drove away.

Sydney waited in the parking lot to see if anyone else came out the door. No one did. When the school opened, she entered, found his name in a sign-in log, and went to the room he'd indicated as his destination. It was a machine shop. She went to each machine, and though they'd been cleaned after use, she found aluminum shavings and small pieces in a waste bin at three of them.

He was making something, possibly parts for a car.

She found a supervisor and asked about after-hours use of the room. The man told her it was possible if a person was a student and familiar with operating the machinery. Sydney mentioned the person she'd followed as someone who'd recommended her. She learned he'd been working lately on a project that was nearing completion.

Sydney followed him again another night, this time in a rented Chevrolet, but this time departed soon after he did. He drove straight home.

"He's not meeting anyone," she told the nervous woman when she called. "He's building something at the tech school, maybe for his car, maybe for you. I suggest you ask to go with him next time to find out."

More calls followed from new clients, and Sydney had a full schedule of cases within just a few months.

She'd learned two things: she needed better computer information tools to conduct such a business, and she would need help.

She also concluded that her new office and occupation far outclassed the 12-year-old Prius she drove. She paid $225,000 cash for a new Kalahari Gold and Rubellite Red Mercedes Maybach S580 with a nut brown interior, then had the Prius towed to the junkyard where she sold it for scrap.

She later visited a used car lot and arranged to borrow any car they had for a day or two. An anonymous rental would be far less conspicuous for following other vehicles than a gold and red Mercedes.

Part Two: Forming Up

CHAPTER 4

Just Walked Out the Door

It was the rhinoceros that got Sydney thinking. In a grassy space near the Metro Technology Center sign, there was a full-sized rhinoceros made largely of hammered and welded garbage can covers. She'd walked up to it, read the accompanying description, and found the artist's initials – RMG – worked several times cleverly into the sculpture like "Nina" in a Hirschfeld drawing.

The school provided Sydney with the artist's name. Across town, she located his workshop, a busy place of hammering, bright flashing light, and showering sparks from a grinder. One person was at work, and Sydney approached him when he put down his tools for a break.

"RMG?" she asked.

"Yes," the man answered with a ready smile. He was in his mid-20s, dressed in work boots and stained coveralls, and had muscular bare arms. "Do I know you?"

"Sydney Bridgewater. I worked for Stansbury Law Firm which administered your grandfather's will."

"The treasure hunt; I remember it well. Is there some problem with that?"

"None whatever. I greatly admire a man who can sit in his home office and grow a fortune to $1 billion with nothing but a computer he knows how to use and an occasional glass of fine bourbon."

Sydney *didn't* mention that another reason for her admiration was she'd wanted to steal a big part of that $1 billion, but said grandfather had always been a few steps ahead.

"Then, if you came to chat, let's go out in the sunshine."

"Perfect," Sydney replied, and they carried folding chairs out of the metal shed to a spacious grassy yard.

"So, what's up, Ms. Bridgewater?" asked Rory Michael Griffith.

"I'd like us to figure out if you could work for me."

"Hmmm, you do see I'm kind of busy here."

"Impressively so; it was your rhinoceros that brought me."

"That's Pugsy, temperamental and quick to argue. I'm afraid she's not for sale if you were wondering."

"Do you have other work like that," Sydney asked.

"Nothing so huge. I have a bunch of smaller things sitting around gathering dust and cobwebs. People who want to buy something track me down and pick through them."

"How long have you been doing this?"

"Six years or so since high school," Rory replied. "I learned to weld there and at the trade school and kept at it. It's not much of a living, but it's art, and I enjoy doing it."

"Do you have a gallery to show and sell your work?"

"No, can't afford that. I rent space in this tin building to make the various pieces, but I don't do much to sell them."

"Such a common story with artists," Sydney said. "Great on the artistry, not so much on pricing and selling."

"I got $35,000 for Pugsy," Rory said. "I thought that was pretty good."

"Good for you; that's an excellent price."

"So, what do you do?" Rory asked.

"I worked as a Computer Systems Analyst for many years but now I have my own business as a private investigator. I work on things the police don't get involved with."

"Do I need investigating?" Rory inquired with a relaxed smile.

"Not that I know of," Sydney replied. "I'm here because I'm looking for occasional help in my business. I solve Most cases from my office with computers and common sense. Others require skills I could probably learn but would rather hire. You seem like you might have some of those skills."

"And you'd trade me space in some sort of gallery for my assistance?"

"Exactly, plus $1,000 a day."

"Hmmm, sounds like I should look at this space. I could stop by tomorrow after I've had a chance to clean up."

"Good, here's the address," and she gave him her business card.

Rory appeared in mid-afternoon, fresh-scrubbed and wearing dress pants and shoes and a short-sleeved striped shirt with a collar.

"This is quite the fashionable area," he said. "I drove around the whole business park. There are many big-name companies with offices here."

"It's very upscale," Sydney said with a smile. "That's why I chose it."

"I figured it would be. A fine lady in a proper business suit hardly ever visits my grungy welder's workshop."

"Shall we look around? I have this whole building."

They did so for the better part of an hour. Rory asked lots of questions; Sydney gave lots of answers.

"This place is empty," he observed. "How would we set things up for people to see?"

"There are companies that do staging. They bring furniture and display stands and arrange the room to look good. They'll even come to your workshop and bring all your for-sale items here. If you have an actual "opening" where people come for an evening to look around, there are companies to manage that. We do nothing except point them to the space and let them work."

"And pay the bill," Rory said.

"Yes, and we pay the bill from the evening's sales. That should be easy if we get enough interest."

"Aside from a couple of big scores, my sculptures aren't making me much of anything now."

"How much art do you have?" Sydney asked.

"Maybe 50 pieces. Enough to fill this conference room and one of the offices."

"Then this would work nicely."

"Will the stagers cart everything back to my workshop when it's over?" Rory asked.

"They would, but I thought you could just leave it as a permanent exhibit if there's anything left. It would be for sale and visible by appointment all the time."

"I'm in," Rory said.

Sydney hired a publicity firm to create an "open house" flyer for Bridgewater Galleries. It would be mailed to Oklahoma companies with sales of more than $10 million a year, companies in the office park where she worked, art galleries and their patrons, and the publicity firm's standard mailing list. She gave them Rory's workshop address to obtain pictures of the art.

She then hired a staging company to gather the sculptures, have them cleaned of dust and cobwebs, and set them up for viewing on the first floor of her building. Lastly, she enlisted a catering firm to provide beverages and food for the typical evening where people in fancy dress walked around with a glass of wine and a small plate of nibbly things and looked at art.

When the event occurred two weeks later, Rory spent the evening charming the guests and answering their questions, many of which were asked so the person, commonly a young lady, could spend more time talking to him. Sydney schmoozed about as the newest office park resident, and the 250 or so people who showed up roamed about viewing Rory's art and considered whether to spend anywhere from $5,000 to $75,000 for a welded metal cactus, a steampunk motorcycle, or a pink flamingo made of raspberry soda cans, among many other objects for sale.

Of the 47 items on display, 31 sold for $235,000. Rory was astonished as one piece after another just walked out the door.

"Wow," he said, "I didn't know I had so much stuff sitting around. And I surely wouldn't have dared set such high prices. Thank you so much."

"You're welcome," Sydney replied. "This office park, high-brow atmosphere drives the prices up."

"I guess it must be time to talk about what I can be doing for you."

"I'm not entirely sure at the moment," Sydney replied, "but my work varies from client to client. I do most of it from the safety of my office upstairs, but I can see occasions where I might have to go somewhere and let people find me. I may need to install computers and surveillance equipment, follow electronic trackers, navigate large crowds and shows, and work among people who are often entitled, demanding, and downright creepy. With you along as security, complete with a dark suit, forbidding sunglasses, and a curly wire in your ear, you'd be a deterrent and a comfort."

"Sounds cool," Rory said, "but I know something else to make it even better."

"What?" Sydney asked.

"My sister."

CHAPTER 5

Fashions You'd Let Your Daughters Wear

"Tell me about your sister," Sydney said.

"Sandra lives in Dallas and works as an intern for a fashion designer. I've seen some of the clothing she's created, and she has a remarkable talent for colors and fabrics and, in general, what looks good on a person. I don't hear much from her, so I gather she's swamped."

"She sounds talented."

"Two other things about her might also interest you: she's gorgeous and has a martial arts black belt."

"You're right; I'm interested."

"I'll send you her phone number."

Sydney drove 210 miles south a week later and met Sandra Ellen Griffith for lunch at a downtown restaurant Sandra had chosen. Rory was right; she was lovely and very well-dressed.

"My brother said you worked for the Stansbury firm at one time," she said.

"Yes, for nearly ten years, though I never met your grandfather in all that time. I wish I had. I greatly admired his accomplishments."

"Grandpa Xander was charming once you got to know him. I liked him a lot. He helped us start our family business and left us very well off when he died. Caroline, our mom, was generous in helping Rory and me get started but wants us to make our own way in the world. So that's what we're both trying to do."

"Rory said you got this fashion design internship right out of high school. It sounds like you were a stand-out at an early age."

"That was a real break, and I've worked hard to learn what I need to know and be a credit to my employer."

"What do you do?"

"Everything the shop does is custom, or bespoke, as we say. Clients come in with some vague idea of what they want. We talk with them to find out what it's for – prom, office, party dress, or whatever – and to get an idea of the desired style. We take measurements and make drawings, and once the client approves them, we make whatever's in the drawing to the proper size."

"And you like doing that."

"Yes, I do. What I like about it is turning a client's idea into something real that makes the person happy."

"That does sound satisfying," Sydney said. "You're doing pretty well, I gather."

"I am. The shop where I work in Dallas is bustling and I've progressed to where I can interview a client, make drawings, and create the final piece without assistance.

"But I'm not so sure how Rory is getting on. He's okay, he says, but trying to make it as an unknown artist is tough. His welding work is extremely detailed and presents well, but it's hard for him to convince people it's serious art."

"He's doing a little better now," Sydney said.

"Yes, he told me about the gallery you set up for him and his opening. That was super, but it does leave me with questions."

"I have answers."

"Why would you help an unknown welder of random objects out of a universe of well-established artists? Why would you want him to work for you yet be vague about what he'd be doing? Why did you drive 200 miles just to have lunch with me?"

"It's because of your grandfather," Sydney replied. "He was brilliant in building and managing his fortune and worked to help his children do the same. I have a business with growing needs and opportunities. As grandchildren of someone I admire, I'd like to offer some of these opportunities to you."

"Pardon me for being blunt," Sandra said with a tight smile, "but I think you're being vague again. I don't see how an investigation firm could offer something better than what I have now, doing what I've spent five years learning how to do."

"You told me what you like about your job," Sydney said. "Is there something you don't like about it?"

"I guess the most disappointing thing is some people's taste," Sandra answered. "Occasionally, what they want is so trashy with all these filmy, see-through fabrics and everything cut so low in front and back. It's like they want to see how close to naked they can get. I like creating lovely clothes that make people look beautiful but still allow them to wear underwear."

"I've seen some red carpet dresses and know what you're saying. I like to wear tall heels and short skirts but certainly wouldn't wear anything beyond what is decent."

"Me, either," said Sandra. "That's why I'd name my shop Fashions You'd Let Your Daughters Wear, to warn away people who want trash and welcome those with good, or at least respectable taste."

"So, here's something to think about," Sydney said. The building I lease and occupy has about 7,500 feet^2 of empty offices. How would you like to open your design studio in some of that space?"

Sandra looked surprised. "I've thought of someday opening a shop to make fashionable clothes for young women, the kind all their friends would want too. Just a part of that space would be plenty for me to work and have a couple assistants. Working closer to home would also be nice, but it sounds like an expensive start-up."

"Maybe not so much," Sydney said, "cutting tables, upscale sewing machines, material storage racks, and other furniture. It sounds like you could get going for under $75,000. There's already a showroom where Rory had his opening and a place to work with clients. I'd give you free rent for three years. Seems reasonable, don't you think?"

"Maybe so, but what about me working for your private investigator business? How would that fit in?"

"That would be now and then for maybe a few days. The rest of your time is just that: yours."

"At $1,000 a day, Rory told me."

"True story."

"Like you said," Sandra replied, "it's something to consider. Having my studio and assistants would be wonderful. The $75,000 would be a stretch, and here I apologize for being too presumptive, but perhaps you could also lend that to me with no payments for three years."

Sydney smiled and nearly laughed out loud.

"Sandra, I can see you are a good businesswoman and also an

excellent negotiator. I would loan you start-up money with three years of no payments or interest."

It was a month before Sydney heard from Sandra.

"If your offer is still open," she said, "I'm ready to say yes."

"Then come see the building layout and figure out how you'd use it."

Sandra showed up on a Friday afternoon. Sydney toured her through the three upstairs offices and the space available downstairs.

"This is the building's conference room," Sydney said. "I use it and the furnished office next to it as Bridgewater Galleries. You see a halfdozen of Rory's sculptures sitting about, which is what remains of the original collection he brought and new ones he's since made. You can re-purpose this room as a gallery of fashions you design. You might want an opening like Rory did when you're ready to start your business."

Sandra looked eager to begin. She found a large table, set up to work, and for the remainder of that day and well into the weekend she measured the available spaces and made room layout drawings. By Sunday noon, she'd prepared a complete list of needed furniture, machinery, and shelving, along with drawings of where it would go. She showed it to Sydney before departing.

"Some of these tables must be custom-made because of their size, and a couple of the machines will take several months to get," Sandra said. "I'm guessing it'll take about two months to get everything in place and another couple weeks to design and sew samples for display in the gallery. Then we'll be ready for an opening."

"Sounds great to me," Sydney replied. "Do you need anything else from me?"

"No, I believe we're good. I'll be able to cover the $75,000, I think. It might even come in somewhat less."

"Then go forth and prepare for a new life adventure. I'll be happy to see you in operation."

CHAPTER 6

Cab Drivers and Bartenders

Sydney's office building front doorbell rang, and one of her computer screens showed two policemen waiting. They didn't look impatient or sinister, but their visit was a curiosity.

"Welcome, officers," she said as she buzzed them in. "I'm upstairs to the left."

The computer was the first thing they saw as they entered.

"What is this, NASA?" one said, sounding surprised. "You have more computer power here than we do at the station."

"I have enough for now," Sydney replied, waving them to chairs. "What can I do for you?"

"You are Sydney Bridgewater PI?" one asked.

"I am."

"Do you have a certificate saying you've completed PI school?"

"I do."

"Then the school acquainted you with the types of cases you should be working on."

"I was so informed."

"Good," said the second officer. "We just wanted to ensure you knew not to get involved in active police investigations. Sometimes those investigations go on for a long while and are confidential. Having somebody stir around in them can ruin months of painstaking work."

"I understand," Sydney replied. "Have I interfered with you in any way so far?"

"No, you have not, and we appreciate that. We were also wondering how big an operation this was, and did you take up this whole building."

"No, it's just me in this office, finding lost grandfathers and straying husbands."

"Then we'll leave you to your work," said one.

"Thanks for your time," said the other, and they found their way out the front door.

The phone rang an hour later. Then it rang again a few hours after that. It was the same in the days following. After each call, she would search her computer for something, or leave the office to seek out something in town, or make a few calls herself, then contact the client with an answer. It was a solitary job most of the time. But there were times she needed help.

A late afternoon caller identified herself as an assistant to a local attorney and asked if Sydney could serve notices to individuals around town.

"How many notices?"

"There are 63 of them, and they need to be done in three days."

'Yes, I can do it. They'll cost you $125 each because of the short notice."

"Wonderful, you're the only one I've found who would do them at all. Can you pick them up yet today?"

Sydney said she would and got the address, then called Rory. He agreed to help, and the two of them got the job done in the requested three days.

She called Rory again a week later.

"Another job?" he asked.

"Yes, a furniture store downtown. They think someone is getting in at night and stealing art off the walls, candle holders off tables, and other small decorative items like lamps and pillows. They want some surveillance cameras set up."

"I can do that."

"If I give you the address, can you just go there and take care of it yourself?

"Sure."

Rory did so and was done a day later. The thief turned out to be someone who once worked there, still had a door key, and knew the alarm codes. He wasn't selling the items he stole; they were all neatly stacked in a storage unit. He just enjoyed the thrill of sneaking in somewhere and taking something, whatever it happened to be. Sitting in his storage unit reminded him of all the times he'd done so, and was pleasing to him.

Sydney strongly recommended that the store change locks and alarm codes now and then, leaving it up to the manager to turn the thief over to the police.

A month later, a woman called saying her boyfriend had stolen her motorcycle.

"When did this happen?"

"Two days ago. I called police and they said I should wait. He'd likely bring it back."

"And you don't think so?"

"No, he left a note saying he wouldn't return and I shouldn't come after him. 'Rosebud is mine,' the note said. He thinks the bike is his, that I gave it to him. I didn't."

"He called it Rosebud?" Sydney asked.

"Yeah, he grew up in Rosebud, a small community in Texas. It's about five hours south of here."

"Do you think he might have gone there?"

"Possibly, friends and family, maybe."

"Do you want to go find him?"

"I don't want to chase after him, but I do want the bike back. It's a Harley, and I waited nearly a year to get it."

"How about I go look for you? Do you have pictures of him or the bike?"

"I have both, but I can't pay you hundreds of dollars an hour."

"The road trip is on me," Sydney said. "If I get your bike back, it'll be $1,000."

"Then yes, please go find it."

Sydney called Rory from her car.

"Can you ride a Harley?" she asked him.

"Yes, I can, and I'd love to. When do I leave?"

"Tomorrow morning, and we have to find the Harley first."

They drove south to Rosebud in Sydney's Maybach, looked around town for a while, then went to a bar.

"Cab drivers and bartenders know everything," Sydney said.

"I'll file that away," Rory replied.

They got a hit at the fourth bar they tried.

"He was in here yesterday," said the bartender. "Said he was heading to Temple for a movie today. Talked a lot about his new motorcycle. Shouldn't be hard to find him in Temple."

They drove there and checked lots of the two multiplex theaters in town. Rory spotted the bike in the second one, so they parked and walked to it. Sydney sat on the bike as if she were in a Harley Davidson showroom.

"We'll just wait for him," she said. "How long could a movie last?"

Another 35 minutes, the answer turned out to be, because that's when a man who looked just like the picture Sydney had walked toward them.

"That's my Harley," he said.

"Actually, it isn't," Sydney said. "It belongs to the woman you took it from, and unless you want police to come take it away, and you along with it, you'll give me the keys right now."

His protestations went on a short while; then he finally surrendered the keys.

"How do I get home?" he asked.

"Talk to the hand," Sydney said, showing her upraised palm. She gave the keys to Rory.

He was soon on the road headed north into gathering darkness. One of his childhood dreams had just come true – not owning a motorcycle and being a biker, but driving one through the night sitting behind a piercing beam of light.

Sandra called Sydney a week later. She had gone forth as directed, prepared for her latest life turning point, and was ready to open Fashions You'd Let Your Daughters Wear. Once she moved in and furnishings and equipment were installed, she prepared samples of seven outfits she'd designed, and she and Sydney engineered an opening like the one held for Rory. They welcomed 340 people of all financial means, and Sandra walked among them accepting compliments graciously and answering questions. The evening filled Sandra's appointment book for the following two months.

"Do you like sports?" said the voice on the phone. It was Sandra.

"Not the usual ones," Sydney replied.

"Since I'm new to the area, I signed up for a martial arts competition," Sandra said. "I thought maybe I'd meet someone interesting. Rory said he'd be there. Want to join us?"

"Yeah, it sounds like fun."

Sydney watched the event with fascination. Sandra was confident in her moves, fierce and even savage in competition against total strangers. Though she didn't win the grand prize, she acquitted herself well.

"You were terrific," Sydney said when it was over.

"Thank you," replied Sandra. "I like to keep in shape. So, what kind of sports *do* you like?"

"Roller Derby."

"Oh, like 'The meanest hunk o' woman that anyone ever seen,' that roller derby?"

"I fell in love with a Roller Derby Queen," Rory sang from the Jim Croce song.

"I like the names skaters come up with," Sydney said. Jane Reaction, Molly Cule, Anna Phalactic, Polly Nomial, Ava Gadro (jersey # 6.022), and they're all real names; I checked the national registry."

"That's impressive," said Rory.

"And you thought Roller Derby wasn't an intellectual sport." They parted with a hearty laugh.

Sydney was pleased. Thanks in part to her assistance, two people who'd now become close friends were flourishing and enjoying their lives.

She checked Step 2 off her plan.

CHAPTER 7

Something More Going On

C. Monica Stansbury was beginning to think she'd made a mistake. She'd agreed to act as counsel for an international business group known as We Remember, but something about them now seemed – to use a complex legal term – fishy.

C. Monica was a practicing attorney of high regard and owner and chief manager of the Stansbury Law Firm. Stansbury Law consisted of nearly 50 attorneys representing a full spectrum of specialties, all working in a building C. Monica owned. Attorneys were free to solicit and manage their cases without her interference and could seek her advice, but were subject to being enlisted if one of her cases, or any other, needed an intimidating "army" to appear in court. C. Monica managed high-profile matters, such as the administration of complicated and exacting terms specified in the $1 billion estate of Xander Moorhouse. She now served as attorney to each of his heirs.

We Remember's current mission is to manage The List, a compilation of names of specific individuals all over the world whose abilities or talents were of possible benefit to the ongoing operation of We Remember. Stealing skilled personnel by making more appealing offers was a standard business practice, but disturbingly, many individuals named on The List were alleged criminals.

C. Monica suspected something more going on, but aside from recusing herself as counsel, and with no basis to report anyone, and no specifics to make accusations, she was at a loss to make any serious move. She hadn't thoroughly done her usual diligent homework and now it made her nervous.

But there was a way to resolve the matter: Bridgewater Investigations. This organization was new on the scene but its website showed a picture of someone very familiar.

So, she called Sydney.

It had always worked before.

They met in C. Monica's office. It had the same precisely organized reddish-wood desk, Sydney noted, the same grey linen draperies and random art on the walls, and the same vase of fresh flowers – today it was daisies – on the credenza.

"Hello," Sydney said, maintaining a pleasant, neutral expression.

"Welcome," C. Monica replied, "please have a seat." Sydney did so.

"If you don't mind," the attorney continued, "let's first get the awkward part of the conversation out of the way."

"I didn't bring an elephant," Sydney said, "so go right ahead."

"I was disappointed you stole from me, amazed at how much you took, and astonished we never noticed," C. Monica said. "When your attorney, Quentin – such a brilliant man he is – explained you were seeking resolution, it was the first anyone here knew about it.

"The key to easy handling of the matter was you initiating contact with us. Here you were, saying sorry for something we knew nothing about. The remarkable details that later unfolded served only to verify how smart it was to hire you in the first place. And the free advertising your Internet treasure hunt gives us has more than made up for whatever amount you stole. In fact, I've had to hire more attorneys to keep up."

"I'm pleased to hear that," Sydney said, "the hunt is still going on and likely will for some while." Her expression slowly softened to one of relief.

"I'm wondering how things have gone for you," C. Monica said. "I gather your time in North Dakota was profitable."

"Extremely so, and the work was surprisingly interesting. But the winter weather got to be too cold for me. I had to return home or the closest place I have to one."

"Did you make any interesting new acquaintances?"

"Not really. I'm rather much a solitary person, as you may remember."

"What I particularly recall is your beautiful handwriting. Don't you have a collection of vintage fountain pens?"

"I do, 296 of them now. I'm always looking for others but have about run out of places to buy them. Turns out it's a fairly costly, slowmoving hobby at this stage, almost as expensive as collecting shoes, but fountain pens don't take up as much space."

"Very true," C. Monica said. "So, let's move on to why I called you. I wouldn't expect you to need a regular paycheck, so please consider what I propose as an opportunity to do something interesting, creative, and perhaps even moderately adventurous. You can also help me escape some trouble I may have gotten into."

"It's hard to imagine you in trouble," Sydney said, leaning back in her chair. "You are always so thorough and methodical."

"Maybe not so much this time. I've become counsel for the international organization We Remember, based in London. The group sounds genuine enough; its seemingly well-intentioned mission now is to work a list of individuals somehow believed to benefit its interests. But they say they've been unable to locate them. It's as if they all just disappeared. They've authorized me to hire someone who can find them. I believe you'd be good at this, at least according to what it says on your website."

"I very likely can find them," Sydney replied. "This Private Eye business is turning me into quite the busybody."

"But here's where things get a little strange," C. Monica continued. "The List contains many names of suspected criminals. On top of that, We Remember doesn't intend to turn these people over to authorities; it wants to employ them, or so they say. They think these people's skills, whatever said skills might be, could somehow be useful to the organization."

"Sounds pie-in-the-sky to me," Sydney said.

"It gave me a wishful thinking feeling as well," C. Monica said. "In any event, when you locate someone from The List, they want you to bring her or him to London for an interview with someone from the We Remember staff. They'll determine whether the person is a good candidate and decide what to do next."

"Curiouser and curiouser," Sydney said.

"Think about it and let me know if you're interested."

"I certainly will," Sydney said. "It sounds fascinating, yet at the same time, not so much. I'll do some research on it. But before I go, I have one thing to tell you and one thing to ask of you."

C. Monica waited in silence.

"I have two assistants at Bridgewater Investigations my website doesn't mention, namely, both of Xander Moorhouse's grandchildren: Rory and Sandra."

"Goodness, how did that come about?"

"I sought them out and made them both attractive offers. They're continuing their chosen life work most of the time and are available to help me occasionally."

"I see no problem with that," C. Monica said. "What ventures are they into these days to keep busy?"

"Sandra is a fashion designer who recently opened her studio here in town, and Rory is a welder of high-end decorative artifacts. Both have outstanding skills."

"Excellent, I'm sure they will work out well for you. And there was something you wanted to ask?"

"I would greatly benefit from using law enforcement data systems. Specifically, access to Interpol and FBI databases for fingerprints, DNA, facial recognition, motor vehicles, travel documents, stolen property, worldwide traffic camera networks, and airport surveillance cameras would dramatically expand capabilities I have now."

"I think you'll find what you need in here," C. Monica said, handing her a small flash drive, "but from what I gather, you do pretty well on your own."

Sydney spent a day reading what C. Monica provided.

First, she found letters of authorization to access law enforcement database systems. Some involved purchasing a separate computer, so she immediately submitted requests and advance payments for everything she thought she could use.

Next, she found a copy of The List itself. Each individual was identified by a simple reference name like *Quincy* or *Geraldine*, along with an occupation, reasons the person was on The List, and a last known location if there was one.

There was scant information on the We Remember group itself. She found a current member list but no biographical information. No matter: in an hour or so, she'd searched for and found enough information to get started.

She continued to work steadily for several days, developing a sense of the individuals on The List. She produced correlations by age, location, skills, and so forth, and summarized her findings. She then scheduled a follow-up meeting with C. Monica.

"What have you learned?" the attorney asked.

"There are 78 names on The List. Among those, a few may be related in some way, primarily by whereabouts and time period. Not everyone can be pinned to a particular location. Some operate only in vone place, but others show up all over."

"You are interested in the job, I take it," C. Monica said.

"I am," Sydney said, "but before I go much further, how do we get paid, and how will expenses be handled? It's not just me working now."

"I've never discussed it with We Remember."

"Then, to respond to your suspicions, let's see how serious they are. I'll charge them $250,000 for each name identified, located, and brought in for their interview. Expenses will be $3,000 per person daily, no documentation required."

"I'll let them know," C. Monica said. She never even blinked at the amounts.

It took nearly a month to get the new software tools installed and working and for her to learn to use them. That complete, she prepared multiple searches for whatever she could find on the entire list of 78 names. Results came in sporadically over the next day or so and she organized them by each case's coded name. Some had a history a yard long; others barely had a history at all.

It was a good starting point.

Part Three: Rounding Up

CHAPTER 8

This Wonderful Welcome

"How's your work going?" Sydney asked in a meeting with Sandra and Rory.

"As I'm sure you know, the opening was extremely successful," Sandra said, "I got orders for 63 outfits. Fashions You'd Let Your Daughters Wear started with a bang, that's for sure. I've had to bring on an assistant to get orders done on schedule. If they keep coming in as they have been, I will need even more help."

"With such success, you'll probably have many eager applicants."

"Oh, dozens for sure, and thanks to your suggestion to double all the prices at the outset, each outfit is very profitable, which allows us to up the advertising, which brings even more people looking for work."

"Excellent. What about you, Rory?"

"I sold most of what I had. I bring new things over occasionally, and they go pretty fast. The locked doors on your building hardly slow people down at all; it just makes my stuff seem more exclusive. I've even taken two commissions for custom science-fictiony figures."

"That all sounds great," Sydney said. "I have some new work also, and like you, I'd like to make an impressive start. But I'm going to need your help."

"I'm in," Rory said.

"What kind of help?" asked Sandra.

"The job itself is to track down a bunch of people who have been very difficult to find. The first one is an international jewel thief. Can you free up a week to travel?"

"Where to?" Sandra asked eagerly. "Let me guess: an orthodontist convention in Pavement Narrows, Ohio, to find a 93-year-old dentist with a crate of stolen gold.”

“Not this time, but to Italy and Milan Fashion Week.”

“I don’t know what that even is,” Rory said.

“Oh, fabulous,” Sandra said. “I’d love to go there. It would be a marvelous experience. But know we’re here to help you wherever you go. Our businesses will survive with us gone a week or two.”

“So, what are we doing?” Rory asked.

“Here’s what I’m thinking. You’ll be along as my private security. You’ll need matching black uniforms that immediately look formidable and expensive. I’ll need pampered princess clothes for attending the shows and various hoity-toity gatherings and being generally conspicuous. Maybe you could take me shopping once we get to Milan.”

“You’ll also need something elegant to get there, so we should shop for that here. Just who are you going to be?” Sandra asked.

“Excellent question: for the next week or so, I’ll be Lady Ingrid Macalister Seton-Hargreaves, a garrulous society aristocrat known to travel with much ostentatious jewelry. The three of us will do our best to get that jewelry stolen.”

From The List:

Rachel

Occupation: unknown.

Wanted for: jewel theft.

Known only by reputation; never seen

or apprehended.

Last seen: suspected to be based in Italy.

Sydney had arranged her law enforcement database computers to the right of her nine-screen wall display and had begun calling the entire collection *Snoopers*. In the days before her meeting with Rory and Sandra, she'd put them all into deep search mode to find any scrap of information even remotely connected to Rachel. And that's what she got: scraps.

Rachel's lifestyle and work method was to remain unseen and invisible – no clues left behind, no pictures to identify her, no media articles, and no suspicious behavior to spark unwanted interest. She mysteriously appeared where she was least expected, knew precisely where to look for what she sought, and did so quickly, then vanished to disperse it for sale in an underground of anonymity. More than one attempt had been made to find her, to flush her out from whatever dense cover she was bunkered down in, all with no success.

Sydney, Rory, and Sandra arrived in Milan two days before the event began.

The city's history goes back to a Celtic settlement in 400 BC. The Romans conquered it in 222 BC, and it later became the capital of the Western Roman Empire. As the Empire declined over subsequent centuries, the city was invaded by many different groups, including the Visigoths, Huns, Lombards, Spaniards, and Austrians, before becoming Italy's industrial and commercial center as well as sharing the title of world fashion capital with Paris. Winters in Milan (November to February) are in the 0°C - 10°C range and summers (June to August) can be suffocatingly hot with high humidity and temperatures above 30°C.

"How does a fashion show work?" Rory asked.

"There are about 70 designer presentations which take place one per hour from 9 AM to 9 PM over six days," Sydney said. "Since Sandra is officially a fashion designer, I got tickets for the presentations and even some afterparties."

"Will we attend all of them?" Sandra asked.

"Probably not. We can pick designers from the schedule who sound interesting. For example, if you're curious about what Dior, Gucci, or Salvatore Ferragamo have in mind for people to wear next year, those are the ones we'll go to. The main idea is just to be seen – but in a crowd of a few hundred other people who are also here to be seen. It's why I'm bringing a personal security detail with me, to be overly noticeable.

"Meanwhile," Sydney said, "we have plenty of work before things start."

"Yes, we have shopping, Lady Ingrid," Sandra said. "Let's go dress you up as a princess."

They were accommodated in a three-room suite. Rory had a suitcase full of electronics to be installed throughout, consisting of tiny cameras to give overall and close-up views of the rooms and devices to communicate with his phone and computer. Figuring this Rachel person would be skilled enough to find and disable such things, he implemented two separate circuits, one which would be activated by movement and could be found if you were looking for it, the other, not so easily found, which would turn on if any part of the first circuit was disabled.

Sydney had salted the Internet with backstory articles on Lady Ingrid Macalister Seton-Hargreaves, going back seven generations to dilapidated castles and ancestors fleeing their home country with invading barbarians in pursuit. Should anyone wonder who she was, they'd find more than a dozen references that would give her the needed credibility, if anyone believed it.

Located in the heart of Milan, Via Monte Napoleone, Via Della Spiga, Via Manzoni, and Corso Venezia are the streets that make up Milan's fashion district devoted to luxury shopping. Via Monte Napoleone is home to over 20 fashion houses, including Versace, Alberta Ferretti, Prada, Dolce & Gabbana, and Celine. Sydney and Sandra walked from shop to shop along it.

"I've been curious about something," Sandra said, "or maybe I'm just being nosy. Do you have a boyfriend?"

"I do not."

"Have you ever had one?"

"Yes, it was the thing to do in high school, but one was enough. I prefer to spend my time alone without anyone distracting me and cluttering my space. I've never been a mom, divorcee, or widow, and that's just fine with me. My work, whatever it happens to be, is much more interesting."

"I feel the same. My mom was married twice, but she never had much good to say about the experience. Rory and I grew up without a dad, which wasn't great, but Mom did her best to fill in. I find my work fascinating and wonderful, so don't feel like I've been permanently damaged."

"So, yay for us," Sydney said as they entered the next store.

When she and Sandra returned from their shopping adventure, they found about $40,000 worth of upscale daywear, cocktail dresses, and designer shoes, all suitably altered to fit and delivered to the hotel in elegant designer boxes and garment bags. Two outfits for each of the six days filled the available closet space and looked elegantly befitting of someone calling herself Lady Ingrid.

Sandra attended to the jewelry, which consisted of seven exquisite diamond necklaces and assorted bracelets, brooches, and pins. It was all rented and essentially fake, a fact that could only be revealed by a jeweler's magnifying glass. Everything had locator circuitry that linked with Rory's computer. Each set had a locking box, and Sandra secured all seven in the room safe. Rory had kept busy all the time they were gone and continued his work into the night.

Sydney and Sandra, both dressed in character, spent time the next day wandering about the hotel. Lady Ingrid looked and sounded regal in a misty blue Alberta Ferretti caped dress and stiletto heels clicking on the marble floors. Sandra looked especially severe in sturdy black oxfords suitable for running the 100-meter dash, black suit with trousers, white shirt with black tie, dark sunglasses, and a curly wire in her ear that led under her collar.

They located the presentation room with the long runway down the center and chairs being placed on either side, then found a café for what turned out to be an unexpectedly huge lunch.

"We're ready to go," Rory said when they returned. He gave them instructions for accessing the system on their phones and they did so.

"What you see is the system displaying the view from one camera then the next on round our rooms. You can stop at any time and zoom in or out.

"If a camera is disabled," he reached behind a wall sconce and did so, "the system switches to the second set of cameras and continues. If something moves in any room, your phone vibrates and shows the place of movement on the screen. Then you can see who is doing what. Everything the cameras see is recorded live to cloud storage."

"Marvelous," Lady Ingrid said. "There's no guarantee Rachel will even show up for this wonderful welcome, but I hope she does."

A large crowd had gathered outside the presentation room the following day by the time Lady Ingrid and her entourage appeared. They were industry insiders, pop stars, top models, wealthy clients, and various fashion editors, photographers, and journalists. All were dressed in their finest. Some wore exotic name-brand dresses, some wore oversized blazers and slouchy trousers, and a few also wore elaborate hats and veils. They all looked like they considered themselves quite remarkable. Some of them probably were.

Lady Ingrid Macalister Seton-Hargreaves blended in with her pale pink jacket and pants, red ruffled blouse, and standout diamond necklace. The only ones who looked out of place were Sandra and Rory, and given their stern and unsmiling appearance, no one was going to take issue with them.

Lady Ingrid took her assigned seat in the second row from the runway; Sandra and Rory stood attentive on the perimeter. Soon the show began and a model walked briskly down the runway, stood posed at the end, then walked back as the next model appeared. This continued through the first hour, then the designer of that fashion collection appeared onstage to a round of polite applause, after which the next hour's presentation began.

Rory took more interest in the pageant than he initially thought he might.

"Why do the models look so bored and grumpy?" he said into his microphone, "they're all very pretty."

"They maintain a neutral expression to not detract from what they're selling: the clothes," Sandra replied into hers. "This is one place where smiling doesn't sell. But yes, they are pretty. Do you think they might be a little out of your league?"

"Different planet is more like it, unless they like this Blues Brothers vibe you and I have going."

"Well, we do have sunglasses, but it's a long way to Chicago."

"Some of these fashions are bizarre," Sydney said after the second round. "Do you want to stay for more?"

"Absolutely," Sandra said, and they stayed through the morning and part of the afternoon. Their phones buzzed when the hotel maid entered their rooms and Rory watched while she cleaned, made beds, and fluffed things up. She did nothing suspicious, like scan for electronics or fiddle with the safe, so there was no apparent cause for concern.

"Anyone interested in a tour?" Sydney asked. "There's gobs of famous artworks and the usual assortment of historic buildings, and we can get dinner. We'll have to dress down to blue jeans and sneakers to blend in with the locals."

"Sure," Rory said.

"We've seen only a small part of the fashion district," Sandra said.

"I'm up for more of it."

"Didn't you get enough of that today?" Rory asked.

"Plenty, but we're here, so let's go see."

Rory checked the electronics when they returned to the rooms, and Sandra checked the safe. All was seemingly well.

CHAPTER 9

We're Being Robbed

The following day went much the same: more designers, more models, more outfits ranging from the baggy to the diaphanous to the bewildering. They attended an afterparty in the evening, which, of course, involved a complete change of outfit. Fashion was fashion, after all. Lady Ingrid was well-prepared and changed into something as stunning as she'd just worn, but Sandra and Rory kept the same don't-mess-with-me black to emphasize their presence.

Lady Ingrid unhesitatingly joined a group of seven people, one of many such clusters chatting and daintily sipping glasses of white wine. The conversation paused as she did so, and one of the gentlemen said:

"I'm sorry, but your name is so long I don't remember all of it."

"It's Lady Ingrid Macalister Seton-Hargreaves, but Lady Ingrid will do. I'm actually from the USA, but the family has its roots in one of those freezing, far northern Baltic countries."

"Sounds like you have some interesting stories to tell," said a lady in a gold blazer.

"I do, but I don't know how many are true. My favorite is of greatgreat-something Eugenia who was chef for a madman ruler of … Estonia, I think it was. When he was overthrown by the next madman in line, she posed as a fortune teller and escaped by train with a traveling circus. She took her recipes with her and opened a restaurant in southern France when she finally settled down again."

"I think I read a story like that on a restaurant menu somewhere," a man said.

"Very likely you did," Lady Ingrid said. "That may even be where I got it."

"You have these two people in black following you everywhere," a lady said. "Is there some reason for that?"

"Maybe I'm being over-cautious, but someone always threatens to steal the jewelry I wear, which came down from another branch of the family. I enjoy wearing it, so I travel with personal security to keep that from happening."

"They look a bit young for such an assignment."

"They're extremely skilled," Lady Ingram said.

Someone changed the subject at this point, apparently deciding Lady Ingrid had used up her share of the conversation.

Later in the evening, a white-haired man in a grey suit, well on his way to being drunk, put his arm around Lady Ingrid and said: "You and I should go to my room. You're quite lovely."

"No, I don't think so," she said as she texted 911 to Sandra.

Sandra quickly made her way there.

"It looks to me like you're bothering Lady Ingrid," she said to the man.

"Is that what her name is; how interesting. No, I'm not bothering her at all. We're just coming to an agreement here."

"The legal name for it is assault," Sandra said, and before he could respond, she grabbed his arm, twisted it behind his back, frogmarched him across the room, and pushed him into a chair.

"Sit," she said.

"Do you know who I am?" he sputtered, turning red as he tried to get up.

"I neither know nor care," Sandra said, putting one finger on his forehead and pushing him back in the chair. "Stay."

Rory appeared at her side. "Looks like you have this well in hand. Nicely done."

There were gasps and barely suppressed snickers from people standing around Lady Ingrid.

"He sure had that coming," said one.

"He's one of the wealthiest men in Italy," said another. "He tries that often and thinks he can get away with it. Most often, he does."

"Your young lady sure handled him professionally," said a third.

"Indeed, she did," Lady Ingrid replied.

Their phones buzzed twenty minutes later.

"I think we're being robbed," Rory said casually. "Let's watch."

They sat at a small round table and waited for the scene to unfold on their phones. But there was no movement or evidence of anyone in the rooms.

"I don't see anyone," Sydney said.

"Just a moment," said Rory, and he stepped through views from each camera. "Both camera arrays seem disabled, but I also put one in the hallway outside. Maybe we can see something there." The view suddenly brightened to show a figure walking briskly away down the hall.

"That's yesterday's maid." Rory ran the camera in reverse to show the hallway a few minutes earlier. It soon showed the same figure walking toward the room and stopping at its door. She opened the locked door quickly and went inside, whereupon all cameras went dark. They returned to life for a moment, then went dark again.

"She found both my circuits," Rory said. "I guess I'm the amateur here."

"But you got her on the third set walking away," said Sandra.

"Luckily, she didn't find that one." He isolated a full-screen view of the thief's face, got a location from the chip in the jewelry bag, and then sent it off in an email: "Room 879 just robbed of jewelry by this woman. She's heading for the west side entrance."

"Who was that to?" Sydney asked.

"Hotel Security. They have the exits monitored. They wanted in on this because room thefts are bad for business."

Ten minutes later came an answer: "Apprehended, thank you."

"Please hold for me to talk with," Sydney replied.

At the front desk, she was shown an interview room to meet Rachel or whoever she was.

The woman looked at her silently for a moment, then smiled.

"Were you sent to find me, Lady Something-or-Other?"

"I was, and I've been calling you Rachel."

"Rachel, a delicate name for a jewel thief. I like it. You and your ingenious assistants have done much better than others who have tried to find me. I found two of your camera traps, but apparently, there were more. Cleverly done."

"We thought so too," Sydney said.

"What made you think I would be here?" Rachel asked. "I could just as well have skipped it."

"I tried to make it hard to resist."

"You mean by those stories on the Internet? You made those up, didn't you. Ancestors running for their lives when demon hordes attack their drafty castle. Bravo! I should have figured they were fake, but I didn't. They sounded quite entertaining."

"Thank you," Sydney said.

"So here we are," said Rachel. "I should have stayed home, but I didn't. Now what?"

"I want to offer you an alternative: either be arrested by the police and endure whatever that entails or come with me to London for a possible job offer from the company I work for."

"What kind of job?" Rachel asked. "What employer would be enthusiastic about hiring a jewel thief, other than some Charles Dickens Fagin character?"

"I don't know what kind of job. We have to go there to find out."

"You're sure I can't just disappear? I'm good at that."

"So I understand, but no, it's with me to London or the police to wherever."

"The police," Rachel said with a sigh of resignation. "The ever so exhausting and tediously thorough police. They'll dredge up some endless dramatic history of thievery to accuse me of, some of it true, most of it not. That will become a tiresome exercise with far too much publicity. Whatever your London people have to offer might be better, so I'll go along and see how it plays out. I can always run for it if I see a chance."

"We have your picture now, so that may be less of a sure thing than you're accustomed to."

"How encouraging."

"It's only a two-hour flight from here," Lady Ingrid said, rising to depart. "I'll make our reservations."

She found Sandra and Rory. "Are you learning something worthwhile, Sandra? Something that would benefit Fashions You'd Let Your Daughters Wear?"

"Very little in the way of style, but some of the unusual material choices and color combinations might be fun to try."

"Then it hasn't been a waste of your time."

"Oh, not at all."

"I'm off to London now. The two of you can stay as long as you want and find your way home when you're weary of it."

"Well, we're here, as Sandra pointed out," Rory said. "Let's just keep doing what we've been doing for at least another day."

"I'm good with that," Sandra agreed. "But we'll need some different clothes with no Lady Ingrid to protect. Something less intimidating, perhaps."

Historically, a walled settlement founded by the Romans on the banks of the Thames 20 centuries ago is the origin of the City of London. During the third century, Londinium, the name they gave the town, had a population of 50,000, mainly due to the influence of its major port. Greater London today covers 600 miles^2 with a population of nine million.

London is famous for Big Ben, Buckingham Palace, the British Museum, and Tower Bridge. The city is also known for its rich history, double-decker buses, red phone booths, world-class museums and galleries, gigantic lush parks, financial districts, and cosmopolitan vibes.

Once there, Sydney and Rachel went directly to the We Remember front desk and asked for the Board Chairman.

"Do you have an appointment?"

"We do not, but tell him I have Rachel."

The receptionist did so.

"He said you should go right in, but Rachel is to meet with Ms. Goldenrod."

"Welcome to London," the Chairman said. "I see you've brought us someone from our List. Congratulations."

"True enough," Sydney replied, "but if you don't mind, I'd like to know what I'm really doing."

"We're looking for people with well-developed and possibly unusual skills. As you've likely noticed, we've expanded the boundaries of that search to include people who might be considered lawbreakers. I don't want that to hinder finding who we want. As you bring them in, we'll evaluate their intentions through one or more interviews and figure out what to do from there."

"Should I be looking for people in any certain order?"

"Not really," the Chairman answered. "Pick those you find most interesting and challenging to find. I must say that finding Rachel is an impressive first catch."

"It was entertaining, but if there's someone you particularly want next, let me know."

She waited for Rachel in the lobby, who soon emerged from her meeting with a puzzled look.

"What's happening?" Sydney asked.

"I'm off to MI6. My lifetime of remaining invisible gave me enough street smarts to provide practical advice to instructors of new agents."

"What about the jewelry you stole?"

"They'll recover what I still have and settle the rest with the owners and insurance companies. It will be quite a big number."

Sydney joined Sandra and Rory back in Oklahoma City by the end of the week and first handled the backlog of PI cases. Based on the mix of calls, she surmised private investigators would be kept forever busy by nosy, suspicious people who would rather hire someone to ask a few basic questions than ask the questions themselves.

Sandra came to Sydney's office door.

"Hello," Sydney said, "I hear you and your staff busy next door catching up on orders."

"Exactly so," Sandra replied. "My studio got a bit behind while I was gone, which brings me to this check for $15,000 I found on my desk. Six days at your rate of $1,000 a day doesn't come anywhere near that amount. Am I to split this with Rory?"

"No, I rounded up," Sydney said. "Rory got one just like it."

"Your math has a great way of rounding. What about expenses?"

"It was just plane fare, hotel, and food, and my expense allowance covered them handily. As for the $40,000 worth of clothes I bought, I paid for them and still get to wear them if some fancy occasion comes along."

"Then thank you very much. If you need us again, let us know."

Sydney thought back to her meeting with the Board Chairman. What he said to her seemed plausible enough, but there was something slightly off. She wasn't suspicious like C. Monica was, yet there was something there, something she didn't yet see. She would have to pay attention as her job played out.

CHAPTER 10

Just Routine Police Work

Angelina

Occupation: Waitress.

Wanted for: arson, theft.

Suspected of setting fire to popular restaurants in Kirkby,

Everton, and Hunts Cross, each on a Sunday, plus theft of

deposit bag of weekend receipts.

Last seen: London, UK.

Newspaper articles Sydney found in the file gave dates and locations of the fires and estimated damages. Police files attached contained lists of employees at each destroyed restaurant and a cross-reference worksheet showing names of those who had worked at more than one. Notes from subsequent interviews had produced no suspects; everyone had a seemingly solid alibi for their whereabouts on the dates in question.

Pictures of several individuals were in the file but none had aroused suspicion. Police closed the investigation when detectives discovered that the same family owned all the restaurants, that insurance settlements had been substantial, and that insurance companies declined to press charges. Sydney wondered whether there was an Angelina, or if the owners had just torched their least profitable properties.

She ran the 92 employees' and 13 family members' names through Snoopers. This produced lists of those who still lived in the UK, had driver's licenses, and worked in restaurant-related jobs.

Sydney then began an exhaustive review of each suspect. She eliminated those who could not have been involved due to timing and location, then looked for anyone within 100 kilometers of the fires on all three occasions. The top person on that list became the "Angelina" of the moment. Snoopers told the type of vehicle she owned and that she had no current travel documents, such as train or airline tickets.

Sydney assessed the situation.

Police had closed the case, making it ancient history.

Insurance companies had bowed out and would likely raise rates on the owner's other properties.

Any list of suspects was merely that: a list. Only Sydney had any interest in them, which meant there'd be no one to go to for help. She thought it over a while longer, then bought a ticket to London.

It occurred to Sydney during the flight that she was missing something. Police detectives commonly made a timeline, usually on a cork or chalkboard, showing when critical things happened in their case. It had pictures and events arranged in time sequence, sometimes connected by string or colored yarn, together with a hodgepodge of notes and asterisks and arrows, which grew more disorganized by the day but was used to test suspect and witness versions of what happened.

She needed one of these.

She began designing a system since she had full access to her London computer via laptop from her first-class airline seat. She was soon writing code to match the vision in her mind and had a model wholly outlined by the time she landed in London.

Her computer gave locations and phone numbers for individuals on the top-ten suspect list she'd prepared. Using fake We Remember credentials she'd created, she arranged lunch or afternoon tea appointments with each of them. Conversations followed a similar pattern.

"My name is Sydney Bridgewater, and I'm associated with the organization We Remember based here in London."

"Hmmm, never heard of it."

"I follow up on police and other matters that are seemingly unresolved."

"You're police?"

"No, but they're aware of what I do."

"Unresolved, you said. What would that be?"

"Do you recall that series of restaurant fires in the news about a year ago?"

"I saw mention of it on the TV, but that's all been settled. Police closed it, I heard."

"Yes, they did, but there are still a few questions."

"Well, I don't have any answers or questions either. Done is done as far as I'm concerned."

The potentially helpful part of the conversation thus never began as the individual ended and sometimes exited the interview. She finished her scheduled meetings over the next two days without getting anywhere.

She returned to the suspect list and expanded it to 20. She turned Snoopers loose to check for anyone showing a noticeable change in lifestyle (two did, but each was from an inheritance), for those who had second jobs or government assistance or obtained frequent payday loans, or those with any history of antagonism with the owning family. This whittled the 20 down to six. She made more calls and more appointments.

She was in Liverpool talking with person number four when she got what she'd been seeking.

"If you must know, yes, I set those fires," said the new Angelina designate. "I did the accounting for the family's accumulation of restaurants and grew weary of listening to the owners complain year after year about how expensive they were to operate and how much money they were losing. So, I burned three of them down. It probably wasn't the most logical solution since it got me fired, but it's history now. Since the police closed the case with no charges filed, no one will arrest me."

"No one is planning to," Sydney replied, and she explained the intentions of We Remember and their need to go to their London offices.

"Why should I go with you? said Angelina. "How do I know you're being straight with me? What if I don't want the job? There are lots of questions here."

"The answers are in London. It isn't that far from here." They flew there the following day.

"I'm here to see the Board Chairman," Sydney said when they arrived.

"Do you have an appointment?" the receptionist asked. "Of course you don't. Whom have you brought us this time?"

"Angelina."

Jimmy Ray

Occupation: truck driver.

Wanted for: theft, counterfeiting.

Suspected of printing US $100 bills on stolen currency paper

and selling it to contacts in South America.

Last seen: St Louis, MO, USA.

Notes in the attached file mentioned two high school boys who had stolen a truck gassing up at a convenience store. The driver had gotten careless and gone to the restroom, then emerged to find his truck gone. Police found the vehicle two miles away on a farm road the following day, and the two thieves were easily identified from a convenience store security video.

No actual harm done, Sydney thought. But there was more. The truck's cargo, ten pallets of blank currency paper, enough to print $1 billion worth of hundred-dollar bills, was missing.

In police interviews, the truck's driver said he was just a driver and never knew what the truck was carrying. The boys admitted to the theft but claimed they knew nothing about the cargo either. They had never opened the truck's rear door. They did reveal they'd been paid to steal the truck and leave it parked at a local shopping center, and the driver's convenient carelessness had made their task much easier, but still maintained they'd never seen the cargo.

Sydney began her investigation with surveillance footage of the shopping center from the night of the theft. She found one frame showing the parking spot empty, another with the truck parked there, and one of someone on a forklift unloading a pallet from it. The forklift showed a grainy, barely decipherable license plate in the picture, but a plate was visible on a truck parked nearby. The two led to a rental agency, and by phone, Sydney got the name of the individual who had rented it that day. He did not live in the area, but she tracked him to an address in St. Louis.

Sydney drove to St. Louis and spoke with the woman who answered the door. She said he'd called the night before from Indianapolis but didn't know where he was now. She referred Sydney to the truck dispatcher.

"I'm looking for Jimmy Ray," she told the dispatcher as if Jimmy Ray was a friend or neighbor. "His wife said he was back on the road going somewhere east."

"He's on his way to Baltimore in a black tractor and trailer. The trailer has a big red rose on it."

"Thanks," Sydney said. She headed that way and caught up at a truck stop in Columbus the following afternoon. She parked near the truck and waited.

"Headed to Baltimore?" she asked when he approached the truck half an hour later.

"Who wants to know?"

"Sydney."

"Looking for a ride?"

"Information."

"About what?"

"Ten pallets of missing paper."

"What kind of paper?"

"The kind you print $100 bills on."

"You a fed?"

"No, a private investigator."

"Don't think I can help you, Ms. Sydney," Jimmy Ray said. "Currency paper is a classified shipment category. It goes in a much smaller truck, and you need an export license to haul it."

"I'm looking for the driver. I might have an offer for him or her."

"What kind of offer?"

Sydney explained.

"Might be interesting, but I'm afraid I can't help you." He got in his truck and drove away.

Sydney knew his destination, so headed east as well. Since a Kalahari Gold and Rubellite Red Mercedes Maybach S580 was not an inconspicuous car, she plotted a route through West Virginia instead of going the shorter way through Pennsylvania. When she arrived, she saw the black semi with a rose in a line of trucks waiting to unload. She parked and climbed up into the truck with him.

"You again," he said. "I didn't see you on the road."

"I went a different way. Any thoughts about my offer?"

"I made a few calls and heard about pallets of currency paper moving to Miami, then on to South America by ship. Might be what you're looking for."

"I'm looking for the driver, not the paper. Since you are about the same build as the person I saw driving a forklift in a surveillance photo, I think it was you. Are you Jimmy Ray? Your wife seems to think so."

"She's correct, Ms. Sydney, I am. I might have some interest in the offer you spoke of. What happens if I say yes?"

"This happens," and Sydney called her contact number in London.

"I have Jimmy Ray in Baltimore," she reported.

"We'll send a plane by morning."

A plane.

They were serious.

"They're sending a plane for you."

"A plane? From London?"

"That's correct. Here's $3,000 in cash. Park your truck and buy some new clothes for the trip. Be at the Baltimore airport in the morning. They'll find you."

"Hold on, hold on just a minute," Jimmy Ray said. "First of all, I'm only unloading half the truck here. The other half has to be in Philly tomorrow. Next, I don't want to park it just anywhere. I need to know it's safe. And then, I have to tell my wife something, but I'm not sure what. I need some time here to get this put together."

"What did you tell her about the currency paper and the counterfeiters?"

"The whole story. She wasn't thrilled about it but was glad I told her."

"Then do the same now. I'll stay with you until everything is settled, then I'll call in the plane."

Ruby

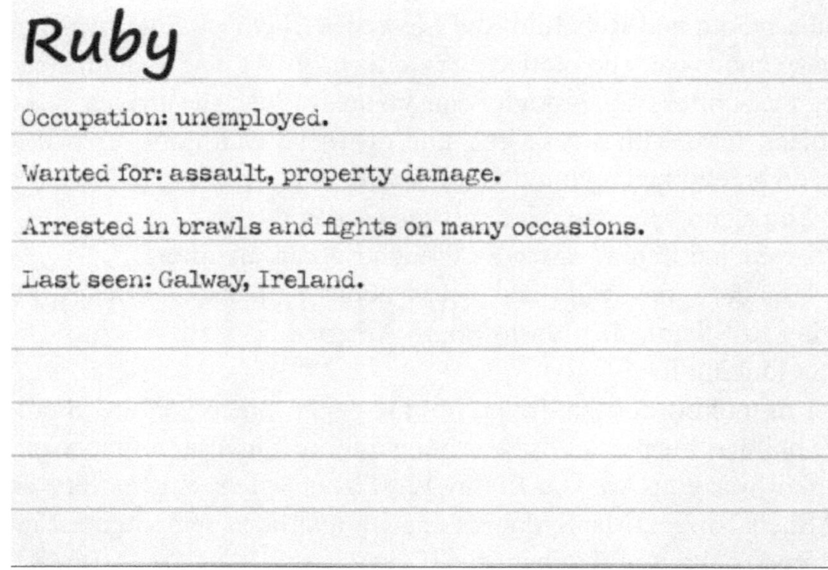

Information in Ruby's file portrayed her as an angry person with no characteristics of a ruby at all. She didn't sparkle or glitter. She wasn't valuable. There was no fire burning in her eyes except anger, but there was plenty of that.

Ruby didn't know what she was angry about. About people who looked at her funny, maybe. About being a loser, maybe. About being disrespected, although she didn't know what she needed to do to gain respect, so settled for beating people up. If people couldn't respect her, they could be afraid of her.

She spent much time recovering from the results of her everpresent negative attitude. She was either in bed recuperating from a hangover or a fight, or she was in jail for being drunk or assaulting someone, or she was at a bar somewhere complaining loudly about what a tough life she had, how she never got a break, and how the system was against her. Knowing this, Sydney figured Ruby wouldn't be hard to find.

Sydney flew 13 hours to Dublin and drove another three hours west to Galway. Arriving in early afternoon, she slept till evening then visited local pubs to ask around. She was eventually directed to Taaffees Pub, a popular bar in Galway City where Ruby often spent time.

Sydney saw no one matching Ruby's demeanor, so she took a stool at the bar and ordered a pint. Three bikers came in an hour later and took seats at a table since the bar was packed. One was loud and already showing signs of too much to drink. It was likely Ruby. After a while, Sydney took a business card from her purse, attached a £100 note, and asked the server to deliver it to the table.

Ruby unfolded the bill and looked around, her gaze settling on Sydney. After staring for a while, she stood up and walked to the bar.

"Who are you?" she asked gruffly.

"Sydney."

"You a cop?"

"I'm a messenger."

"But not a cop."

"No."

"What's this Bridgewater Investigations about?"

"It's me."

"Are you investigating me?"

"I'm looking for someone named Ruby. Might that be you?"

"Yeah, what's the £100 for?"

"To get your attention."

"Why?"

"To see if you're interested in a trip to London."

"Why would I want to go there?"

"I'm working for an organization that wants to talk to you, maybe offer you a job."

"What kind of job?"

"I have no idea. We have to go there to find out."

"Are you going to get me in trouble?"

"Not planning to. But if I do, you look like you can handle it."

"I'll think about it," she said; "thanks for the cash." She returned to her table. By the time she looked back at the bar, Sydney was gone.

Sydney's phone rang the following afternoon. Ruby sounded like her head hurt, a lot.

"London, you said. How you gonna get there?"

"Drive. I have a rental."

"Do I ride with you?"

"You may, or you can find your own way."

"If you don't mind, I'll take my bike so we don't have to talk for 12 hours. And I'll have a way back."

"Suits me," Sydney said, giving Ruby the location. "Meet you there tomorrow evening."

They had dinner together in London, then met at We Remember in the morning. The same receptionist Sydney had dealt with before greeted them. "Ruby, is it?" she asked.

"Yeah," Ruby replied.

"You'll be meeting with Ms. Goldenrod in a few minutes. Sydney, the Board Chairman wants to talk with you. Go right in."

"Welcome to London, again," he said, "You're getting through The List much more quickly than we expected."

"Probably because it's just routine police work. I'm using the same software your local police have or should have. An average detective could do this."

"That wasn't our experience. Our local constabularies are fully loaded with work and don't have the time to specialize. You've already proven good at it and bring intuition and cleverness to the work. You are just what we needed."

"Well, I have 74 names to go, so it looks like we'll be working together for a while."

"I realize it may seem wasteful for you to bring the person you find to London each time, but we want to ensure he or she gets here. It also closes the loop on your involvement; your part is complete. If you have an invoice, we can also pay you."

"That works for me," Sydney said, "is there anything else I need to know?"

"Not now; just keep doing what you've been doing. If we want you to stop or have something else for you to do, we'll say so."

Sydney returned to the lobby. She thought he'd had the perfect opportunity to question the absurd amount she was charging, but he didn't. Apparently, they had tons of money and were more grateful for progress than concerned about its cost. Accordingly, she prepared an invoice for £845,000 for the four individuals she had brought in.

But what might be the something else they'd want her to do?

Ruby came out of her session half an hour later. She was not in handcuffs, not accompanied by a guard, but had a dazed, dumbfounded look.

"You look like you've been hit by a truck," Sydney said.

"I can't believe what they said," Ruby replied. "It took me completely by surprise. They want me to open a bartending school."

"Now *I'm* surprised," Sydney said.

"They'll have someone teach me basic stuff for a month, then get me a bartending job wherever I want to live and pay me to practice and learn it. After a couple years, they'll find a posh building somewhere, outfit it with practice bars, and help me get a school going. They said I'll be doing the world a favor by teaching how to make drinks proper."

"Sounds great," Sydney said. "I guess it was worth coming to London."

"Yeah, for sure. Thanks for leading me to it. Maybe I won't need to get drunk so much."

"Maybe not."

Before heading to the airport and Oklahoma City, Sydney visited Ms. Goldenrod.

"Ruby told me what you plan for her and I'm hoping it works out. I'm wondering what became of Angelina and Jimmy Ray."

"I thought you might ask," the woman said. "Angelina is a problemsolver, though her solutions may not always be practical. We found her a position with Scotland Yard on a White-Collar Crime Task Force. They said, off the record, they needed someone who colored outside the lines."

"Maybe a better use of her skills than burning down restaurants," Sydney said. "What about Jimmy Ray? How does a truck driver become a counterfeiter?"

"He was part of a larger group, and driving was his assignment. He gave MI6 details on how and where the group operated, and they passed the information along to the USA Secret Service. In return, we offered him a high-security truck driving job. For example, military bases and other secret and secure government operations have huge computer rooms with many computers. Whenever they buy a new one, they don't let the computer vendor's techs inside to set it up. Instead, they drive a semi to a remote location, and the vendor sets up the computer inside the truck. Once it's running, a driver like Jimmy Ray delivers it to the secure location. There are many trucks on the road carrying out similar assignments."

"What about his truck and family?"

"We sold his rig for him and are moving his wife and their belongings to London."

Back in her Oklahoma City apartment, she finished coding her Timeline project and began to test it with small amounts of data. She completely redesigned how results were displayed and then ran more data. That led to more changes.

She then recalled the file with all The List's names and accompanying data and loaded that into the Timeline program as well. She had a chart in just a few minutes. It spanned all nine of her computer monitors and showed when each individual entered and exited the picture and events as they happened in between. After another day of refinements, Sydney had results.

First, none on The List had ever worked together in the same place.

Second, in addition to those Sydney flagged as apprehended, there was a second flag for those who were deceased or at least reported to be.

Third, there was a new flag that showed in red if crimes the person had committed were serious, yellow if said crimes were minor, and green if there was no crime at all. This came from code Sydney recently added to evaluate crimes identified by The List.

The predominant color was green.

Sydney was surprised. The List was way more than a rehabilitation program. They *were* looking for specific skills.

CHAPTER 11

A Local Legend

Wilson

Occupation: Construction Worker.

Wanted for: vandalism.

Repayment made, suspect never identified.

Last seen: Jacksonville, FL, USA.

Sydney found the following summary in the We Remember case file:

The suspect Wilson stole a dump truck full of #6 gravel at 3:00 one Tuesday morning, drove it onto a golf course in pouring rain, dug deep, weaving ruts the entire length of number seven fairway, and dumped the gravel in the center of the green. He drove around the green's perimeter for good measure, then returned the truck to exactly where he'd stolen it.

Groundskeepers discovered the damage the following morning, opening day of a popular ladies' tournament. The tournament had already been delayed because of rain, but now there was much work ahead to remove ten cubic yards of gravel from the green and repair damage to it and the fairway. This was accomplished by 2:00 the next morning and the tournament went on.

The golf course manager subsequently received an anonymous payment for $25,000 accompanied by a handwritten note: "Believe me, it was worth it."

Sydney obtained names of players who'd signed up for the tournament. She ran each through Snoopers and sent Rory to Jacksonville to interview course officials and those players.

"This has become a local legend people laugh about," he said upon return, "but it wasn't funny then. The pile of gravel has grown to at least ten truckloads in the tale's telling, and the tire ruts have become deep canyons. As you requested, I talked to about 25 people and have a couple of leads for you.

"One of the groundkeepers was buying a new house then and needed cash to qualify for the loan. The overtime would have helped him accomplish that.

"Several players had suspicious husbands at home who always got upset when their wives went off to play golf, especially for an entire day and evening. Here are their names and current addresses. None of them is named Wilson.

"I also investigated rival golf courses for any feuds that might be going on. I didn't find anything beyond the usual competition."

"Well done," Sydney replied, "thank you much."

Rory's findings supported what Sydney had discovered on her own, namely that the brother of the husband of one of the players worked for a sand and gravel company. His name wasn't Wilson, but she didn't expect it to be. Sydney made a few verifying phone calls and filed the information away. It would keep until she located another person on The List for the trip to London.

Jesse

Occupation: Pushcart vendor.

Wanted for: drug sale and distribution.

Works local fairs, changes residence frequently.

Last seen: Charlotte, NC, USA.

Sydney's review of this file revealed that Jesse had become a fixture at the city's more than two dozen annual festivals, selling her daintily painted angel figurines from a sidewalk cart. She'd even worn a white robe with white tulle wings to highlight her role as the Angel Lady. Figurines sold in a white protective box for $25 each, except those in an identical white box which sold for $400, cash only.

The two boxes were the same, except the pricier one contained a business card bearing the address of a bar in Cincinnati. When the card was dampened, it revealed a different local address on the back. The card's presentation at said address gave the bearer a plastic tube containing two grams of cocaine, but only on the day of purchase. After that, the dark figure in the alley handling the drive-by redemptions was gone.

Jesse appeared to know what she was doing. An arrestable drugdealing transaction involved a person with cash and a person with drugs making a verifiable exchange. There was no such transaction if the participants were miles apart.

This had gone on for about a year until Jesse vanished. Purchasers at her cart had become fewer touristy visitors and more of those who wore dirty sleeveless t-shirts and worn-out work boots. Just watching traffic at her cart, one could tell these were not devoted collectors of angel figurines. Jesse had abruptly packed her white robe and pushcart and showed up two months later in business in Little Rock, Arkansas, then Austin, Texas, then Shreveport, Louisiana, and so on.

Sydney reviewed police complaints throughout the South that matched Jesse's operation and deduced she was currently operating in Tulsa, Oklahoma. Sydney drove there and walked about the event. There was no pushcart vendor in a white robe, but there was a young man in a checked sports coat with white boxes of angel figurines for sale. She approached and began a conversation.

"I think I'd like to buy one of these," she said tentatively. "I saw some like them somewhere in Texas and bought several. They make good gifts."

"Your timing is good," the young man said. "This is the end of the inventory. It's my mom's business, but she died last year. I'm closing everything out this week."

"Oh, I'm sorry to hear that," Sydney said. "This is none of my need to know, but was it sudden?"

"Very sudden. She was murdered."

"I'm so sorry. I didn't mean to bring up sad memories. Let me buy four of these since I probably won't see you here again."

The man picked out four white boxes and put them and a brochure in a bag.

"That will be $100 plus tax," he said.

"Oh, I was told they were $400 apiece."

"No, only $25, but other people have asked. I don't know anything about such a price."

He was lying, Sydney noted. He blinked more frequently and started rubbing his chin. "OK, I'll take these and be done. Thank you."

She removed the brochure from the bag once back at her Tulsa hotel. She dusted the brochure for fingerprints using implements from the crime kit she'd assembled, then remotely sent them and the picture she'd secretly taken of the young man's face off to Snoopers.

The brochure talked about craftsmanship, delicate hand-painting, and the versatility of decoration possibilities, and gave the address of the company that made the figurines. The box for a local vendor's name was blank, but within a short time, Snoopers gave her the young man's name, address, a complete 10-card of fingerprints, and a list of infractions he'd been questioned or arrested for. He was not the dutiful saintly son wrapping up his murdered mom's business as he claimed to be. He'd been on the wrong side of things most of his life.

The information also gave his mother's name which, oddly enough, *was* Jesse. A search on her revealed she'd last lived in Charlotte, North

Carolina, and most certainly was not dead. That, apparently, was the story the man used to move inventory more quickly.

But Sydney still needed something: the business card that came with the $400 figurine. She called Rory and asked him to drive to Tulsa.

"Don't dress up," she said, "wear your welding shop clothes. And don't shave. Go to the local Mall event and find a man at a pushcart selling shiny white boxes. Instead of asking, hand him four $100 bills."

Rory called back the next afternoon. "Got a business card here," he said.

"Great," Sydney replied, "sprinkle water on the back of it."

"Water... there's a puddle in the alley where I'm parked. Just a minute."

"Now there's another address on the card," he said when he returned, and he read it to her.

"Thank you. One last thing: that's probably the regular street address. What you want is the alley behind it. Please find it, drive through it. and tell me what you see. Don't drive slowly."

He called again ten minutes later.

"It's a typical alleyway: back doors, fire escapes, full dumpsters, an empty refrigerator box where someone apparently sleeps. There's a guy sitting on a kitchen chair smoking a cigarette at one of the back doors."

"All right, thanks; now get out of there and bring me that card."

"Copy that," Rory said, and he drove to Sydney's hotel.

"This card is supposedly good only today," she said. "I want the two of us to try to redeem it. I'll drive; you sit in the back seat with a camera and take pictures of the deal taking place if one does. She changed into jeans and a rumpled sweatshirt and they set off in Rory's car.

Some while later, Rory directed her to turn into an alley. She did so and proceeded slowly. The kitchen chair was still in place, though empty, but a shadowy figure was farther down the alley. Sydney pulled up to the figure, whom she recognized as the young man at the pushcart, and handed the business card out the driver's window. He accepted it and gave her a small paper bag. She opened it, held up the cylinder for Rory to take a picture, then drove away.

She returned to her car, then parked to watch the building's front door. Rory parked to monitor traffic in the alley. Two hours later, the young man exited the building and drove away. Rory picked up his trail, and he and Sydney both followed at a distance to a small house near an industrial district. There was much activity in the place, as seen through the windows, as if they were packing to leave. After about an hour, Sydney knocked on the front door.

"So glad to see your mother has recovered from being dead," she said when the man answered. She was visible behind him in the room.

"You followed me; what do you want?"

"I have an offer for you to consider."

"Not interested. Just leave us be and we'll be gone in half an hour."

"What I have is better than dealing with the police."

"Nope, we have everything covered. Just go away, and you'll never see us again,"

"Last chance."

"Goodbye," the man said.

"Very well," Sydney said. The man slammed the door and Sydney went to Rory's car. "Call the police," she said. "We'll just wait here until they arrive."

Police arrived ten minutes later.

"Do we get out of the car?" Rory asked.

"No, just let them follow their procedures."

"I was thinking about this fancy new car of yours. It's classy and elegant and all, but it probably isn't the perfect thing for following people. It's distinctive even in the dark."

"You are right about that," Sydney said. "I've arranged to borrow rental cars for this purpose, but that's in OKC, and we're not."

An officer approached the car once the others were busy in the house.

"Was it you who called?"

"Yes," Sydney answered, "we have pictures and evidence to turn over when you're ready."

"We'll do that downtown when we take your statements."

The remainder of the evening took a predictable path. The suspects, amid continual protestations, were taken downtown along with a bag of evidence from the house. Sydney and Rory were directed to the station where they turned in their evidence. Interviews dragged on for hours as everyone told their story to many different officers. Eventually, Sydney and Rory were told to go but not to leave town.

"You didn't get a chance to offer them the London alternative," Rory said.

"No, and it's just as well. I'm not keen on giving drug dealers escape alternatives."

CHAPTER 12

Poker Isn't About Cards

Gina

Occupation: Gambling house manager.

Wanted for: Questioning regarding business practices.

Operates at the boundary of the law; no verifiable violation.

Last seen: Gulfport, MS, USA.

Sydney spent several hours researching this case and began to wonder why she was needed at all. Gina operated a high-stakes poker game in a downtown hotel and was highly particular about how she did so. No drugs were permitted in the room or hallways outside. No firearms inside either. This was the Genteel South, not the Wild West.

She had a certified hotel bartender on-site preparing drinks from hotel liquor. Food came from the hotel kitchen and was consumed at the playing room's bar, not at the tables.

She had three lovely Asian ladies wearing matching gold sheath dresses and strappy gold heels serving drinks. Each spoke perfect English and had enough martial arts skills to subdue an unruly player, take him down the elevator, and leave him on the sidewalk outside. She also had four dealers managing and keeping the peace at the tables.

Games operated every other night, and the four tables of eight players each were most often full. Players paid a $5,000 nightly game fee if they were there only once, but for further sessions, they also paid a $1 million refundable deposit against potential future losses. Players were encouraged to tip serving personnel 25%.

Gina took in about $2.4 million per month. She did not take a percentage of the pot or winnings – the illegal part of such an operation – but took her share of game fees and tips. She paid her employees, she paid her rent, she paid her bills, she paid her bank loans, she paid her taxes. She had no history of complaints.

So why was she even on The List? She wasn't the least bit hard to find. Those interested in Gina certainly knew who she was and where she was and knew she wasn't doing anything illegal. It didn't sound like she needed investigating, but even so, Sydney decided to do a thorough job of it.

"How would you like to learn to play poker?" she said to Sandra.

"I know a little about it."

"But probably not enough for what I have in mind. Can you make time for a week of poker school?"

"Sure, I can do that."

Sydney hired a former poker champion to teach Sandra various forms of the game. Sandra learned not only rules and procedures but the basics of when to bet, when to raise, when to call, when to bluff, and when to fold.

Most important, she learned about tells. Poker isn't about cards, she found out; it's about understanding your opponents. Players exhibit mannerisms that often vary slightly when they have a winning hand and when they don't. Interpreting those mannerisms helps an opposing player decide what to do next.

Sandra also learned about players who didn't much care about money won or lost but drew their enjoyment from crushing the spirit of other players and watching the hope in their eyes slowly dim and die.

Rory's part of the assignment was to hold the money. He was to sit silently in the game room with a metal briefcase containing $2.5 million in cash. He would pay amounts due, buy Sandra additional chips as needed, and gather winnings into the briefcase at the end. While Sandra would be pleasantly dressed – stylish but not alluring – Rory would be all in black with sunglasses and a curly wire in his ear. When they showed up at the door, one look told you what their roles were to be.

They flew to Gulfport, Mississippi, and an armored car driver met them at their hotel with a briefcase full of cash. The driver would return to retrieve it when the night was over. After a brief time in their rooms, they rode the elevator to the top floor where they were welcomed into the game room. Rory paid the $5,000 game fee and bought $25,000 worth of chips issued in $25, $50, $100, and $500 denominations. Soon, Sandra was seated at a table among players wearing suits and ties, cowboy hats and jeans, long dresses and tall heels, and baseball caps and scuffed leather jackets.

The game began as cards flowed out from the dealer. While everyone tried to mask their tells during the hand by maintaining an unconcerned, relaxed appearance, Sandra fully manifested hers. She pushed her shoes off, then soon wiggled her feet back into them. She tugged at her skirt and collar as if to smooth wrinkles. She blinked. She rubbed her ear and scratched her nose. She pushed her long hair back and tucked it behind her ears.

The playing room atmosphere was that of focused silence interrupted only by the clatter of chips and the soft swoosh of cards. Occasionally, players would sigh with resignation if they lost, give a brief whoop of satisfaction if they won, or bang their heads on the table if they'd gone broke.

Sandra played her cards with hesitant uncertainty, winning some, losing some, and through the evening and into early morning managed to win $54,000. She had Rory book seats for three more games.

The next game night had a similar format and many of the same players. Sandra subtly assessed them as opponents, just as she'd been assessed the game before. Three of the seven others were obviously pros. They were friendly but looked at her as if measuring how long she would last. Two were chatty beginners and not-sosecretly worried about going broke in the first 20 minutes. Another looked stoned and as if he had no idea where he was. He would be playing on raw instinct, probably proceeding toward reckless. The last was a predator who glanced at her with an ill-concealed half-smile as if calculating how long it would take to reduce her to tears.

"Did you bring your own armed security?" he asked.

"He's not armed; the hotel does not permit it."

"Is that wire in his ear connected to anything?"

"The armored car driver parked down the street."

"Then I guess we won't be messing with him," one of the other players observed.

"Or me," Sandra said. "I have a martial arts black belt."

"Well, now that we're through marking our territory," the predatory player said, "let's get started." Even Sandra laughed. Rory did not comment.

Sandra soon began to get the feeling of the game and played more adventurously. She bluffed a time or two, correctly read tells a good part of the time, and was more challenging with her bets.

The stoner began writhing in his chair midway through the night. He looked wild-eyed, began to moan, and dropped his cards on the floor. "You're all cheating," he screamed. "You have cards up your sleeves. You're cheaters!" The sleeves of Sandra's blue dress ended at her elbows.

The game stopped. The three Asian ladies wearing matching gold sheath dresses and strappy gold heels pulled him away from the table, cashed him out, and took him down the elevator. The game resumed in silence, with Sandra down $137,000. She valiantly struggled back to win $83,000 by night's end.

She lost $32,000 on the third night and, on the last night, ended her high-stakes experience by winning $272,000 for a grand total of $377,000. Rory left a $10,000 tip. The armored car driver appeared when called and took the briefcase and its contents away. He would wire the money to Bridgewater Investigations.

Sandra called Sydney from her hotel room.

"Everything you surmised about Gina is true," she said. "She's not violating any law as far as I could see."

"Make a daytime appointment and explain the We Remember choice to her," Sydney said. "She may be looking for a way out."

Rory did so.

"It sounds possibly interesting, but no, I don't think so," Gina said. "I figure I'm good here for another couple years, then I'll have enough to pack up and move to Portugal. I can make a few million last quite a while there."

CHAPTER 13

Nickle and Dime Fees

Rosalind

Occupation: Estate sales manager.

Wanted for: Questionable business practices.

Skipped the country leaving substantial debt behind.

Last seen: Amarillo, TX, USA.

Sydney went to Switzerland for a week to meet with her Dreyfus Bank broker.

"I'd like you to advance me $2 million," she said.

"Walking around money?" he quipped. "Something to stuff between the couch cushions for a rainy day?"

"Something like that."

"You can do this anytime and anywhere from your computer."

"True, but then I wouldn't be in Switzerland."

The broker brought up her account and studied it for a time.

"Your overall balance is $32 million and change, but you don't have that much available cash right now. Many of your investments will pay dividends next month; that should provide enough. Can you hold out that long?"

"Yes, I can, and thank you." She got up to leave, but he continued.

"How's that Internet treasure hunt of yours doing?"

"You know about that?

"Of course, it's a big deal here in Switzerland. There are whole clubs of high school and college kids who work together on it incessantly."

"Just a minute, let me see."

She pulled her laptop from her shoulder bag and connected to her computer in London. A few screen displays later, she had an answer.

"There's been much progress since I last looked in on it," she said. "Many people are getting closer, some in Switzerland, but no one is getting near the prize. But you're right. It is popular. Nearly 3,000 people are on it right now."

"Then good luck to all of them," the broker said.

The $2 million was to fortify her account in Oklahoma City. She sensed a change coming, possibly soon, and wanted to be ready. What kind of change, she had no idea, but it was there in her mind, working toward something.

She'd asked Rory to investigate the Rosalind matter while she was away, and he reported his results when she returned.

"Rosalind managed estate sales for most of western Texas," he said, "but aside from taking the 35% commission quoted in her contract, she loaded on an assortment of fees that jacked up the cost. These included an extra $500 for each vehicle, an extra 5% for anything in a separate building, 5% more for collections of small items or furniture that had to be sold together, extra for care and security of high-value items, extra for determining a starting value for each item instead of setting the opening price each at one dollar, and a wide assortment of similar extras for this and extras for that which cranked up the total fee closer to 55%. The seller would never know about this unless he or she thoroughly read the contract, which often never happened."

"Not exactly businesswoman of the year," Sydney commented.

"It doesn't end there," Rory said. "Rosalind also had a liberal interpretation of what extra fees covered. A stand-alone garage was considered a separate building, even though it was only a sidewalk width from the main house. Vehicles that didn't run incurred extra for towing to the auction site, even though the auction was often held online. Rooms that bore evidence of hoarding were billed extra for sorting and cleanup but were left as is, and so forth.

"It was only when the sale was completed and an itemized list of fees appeared that the seller, originally attracted by the stated low fee of 35%, realized charges were much higher."

"So these extras were in the contract people signed, they just didn't read it," Sydney observed.

"Yes," replied Rory. "She operated her business in this manner successfully for many years until her incessant nickel and dime fees caused the phone to ring less and less, and then not at all. She filed Chapter 7 bankruptcy, agreed to pay her debts but didn't, and skipped the country to some unknown destination without ever clarifying where many millions of dollars of income received over the years were deposited.

"We have a picture of her, a last known location, complaint files documenting her overcharging, records of her traveling to various countries through the years, and a list of people worldwide with whom she did business. The data said she'd been recently seen in Madrid, but based on travel records Snoopers churned out, it looked like she's been wandering all over."

"Excellent work so far, Rory," Sydney said, "What did you do next?"

"I thought she might eventually get bored and continue with her accustomed habits, so I began searching, one likely country at a time, for complaints about criminal behavior like Rosalind's. Complaints were plentiful, but nothing conclusively pointed to her.

"Then, just yesterday, Snoopers coughed up a new reservation she made at a hotel on Grand Cayman Island. She booked a room for a week, so we're flying there the day after tomorrow."

"Sounds great."

The flight to Grand Cayman Island took six hours from Oklahoma City. Once there, Rory scanned local newspapers and Internet sites for scheduled estate sales while Sydney got online to her London office and quizzed Snoopers further. Neither found anything definitive, but they did compile a list of impending sales events. Two were being held online; six others were being conducted on-site over the coming weekend. They perused the online sales and agreed that Rosalind would have organized neither.

They attended the six on-site sales together rather than splitting up the list, figuring travel time between them wouldn't be substantial on an island only 22 miles long.

The main business had been completed at the first three by the time they arrived, and purchasers were loading items into their cars and trucks.

Rosalind wasn't at the fourth sale, the fifth, or the sixth one. They compared sale flyers from all six and agreed that none appeared to be in Rosalind's style.

"She's not here," Rory said, "or maybe she didn't come to do business."

"We've been at this all day," Sydney said. "Let's find a place to eat."

They went to the Grand Old House Cayman and were shown to an outdoor table on a deck looking out over the Caribbean. It was nearing sunset. The sky was working into a lovely picture postcard scene that had drawn vacationers to the island for years. Sydney's phone buzzed midway through dinner.

"Snoopers says Rosalind was just seen at the Panama City airport," she reported. "Also, it shows that to be the last stop on her ticket."

"Missed her," Rory said. "What's in Panama besides a canal?"

"Don't know; I'll look it up," and Sydney began a search on her phone. "Well, this is interesting," she said after a few minutes. "Panama is one of the top retirement destinations if you want to leave the US. It has a low cost of living, tropical weather, good food, friendly people, political and economic stability, and so on. The only big problem is you have to speak Spanish."

"Maybe she's going to settle down."

Sydney's phone buzzed again.

"Snoopers tells me she applied for a Panama driver's license."

"Did the application give a current address?" Rory asked.

"It did. I vote we go there right after dinner."

They drove to the address Rosalind had put on her application and found it in a pleasant oceanfront area of large apartment buildings. Rory rang the doorbell.

"Uh-oh, you look like trouble," Rosalind said when she opened the door.

"Maybe yes, maybe no," Sydney said.

"Tell me about the 'no trouble' side of things," Rosalind said.

"Sorry, but first, a look at the 'yes' part," Rory said. "Substantial evidence says you swindled many of your customers, skipped the US without paying debts you agreed to pay, and violated terms of your bankruptcy agreement."

"Blah, blah, blah, so you say," Rosalind said. "I asked for the 'no' part."

Sydney responded: "I work for an organization that may be willing to offer you a job and pay off your debts as part of the agreement."

"That sounds a lot better. What kind of job are you talking about?"

"I have no idea," Sydney said. "You and I have to go to London to find out."

"And I don't get arrested if I don't like the job?"

"Not in London, but the bankruptcy court will still be looking for you," Rory said.

"Not much of a choice, if you ask me."

"Were you planning to relocate here to Panama?" Sydney asked.

"I was thinking about it. I'd become a Panamanian National after five years of continuous residency and, at that point, could not be extradited. Panama City is a relatively pleasant place with tropical weather. Nothing's very expensive, including this lovely apartment right on the water. Staying out of sight here for five years seemed like an easy thing to do.

"But now I'm not so sure. You – however you found me so quickly – show up in the first week. Who knows who else might track me down and show up in week two. Five years is a long time to jump every time the doorbell rings. The other problem is the language. Here in town, people know enough English to get by, but everywhere else, it's Spanish. After spending just a few days here, I don't think I'd have the patience."

"So maybe my offer sounds interesting?" Sidney asked.

"It's starting to. When would we leave?"

"Be ready to go in two days."

"Does Mr. Bad News here have to come along?"

"He's going somewhere else."

"Where am I going?" Rory later asked.

"Fly to Jacksonville and make the We Remember offer to Wilson, the gravel on the green guy, and the name I marked on your list. If he's interested, bring him to London as soon as possible."

"Will do," Rory said and flew out the following day.

He located the man they called Wilson quickly enough, but the interview was confrontational.

"That was long ago, ancient history," the man said, "and I paid for the damages. Why are you digging this up now?"

Rory explained the We Remember offer.

"You're disrupting my life for no reason … wait …London?" Wilson asked. "I've never been there."

"Here's your chance."

"And it's free?"

"Getting there is," Rory answered.

"If I did, the first place I'd go to is Abbey Road and walk across the street."

"I'd like to do that too. We'd ride the 139 bus from Baker Street," I understand.

"Baker Street," Wilson said. "Another good place. I'm in."

Sydney and Rosalind departed on an evening flight a day later, landing in London on Monday morning. Rory arrived that afternoon with Wilson, who seemed only interested in the chance to see London. The two went at once to Abbey Road … and walked across the street.

"Well, Sydney, who never makes an appointment," said the We Remember receptionist, "whom do you have for us today?"

"I have Wilson and Rosalind. I can also report that police apprehended Jesse, so she won't be coming, and neither will Gina, who is happy doing what she's doing."

"Very well, Ms. Goldenrod will see the two you brought, and the Chairman will see you in half an hour. I presume you also have an invoice for me."

"I don't, but I'll work one up right now."

"What happened in your meeting," Rory asked on their return to Oklahoma City that afternoon.

"The Chairman told me Wilson, also a computer nerd, was being offered a job as fleet maintenance scheduler for HM Coastguard. Rosalind's job offer is in organizing surplus equipment disposal for MI6."

"Don't they already have people in those positions?"

"Dozens, probably," Sydney said, "and many openings as well. The Chairman continues to be pleased with our efforts, by the way, and doesn't seem to care how much it costs."

"How much *did* it cost him, if you don't mind me asking?"

"I gave them a bill for £516,000," Sydney replied. "Since you did much of the work on Rosalind and on Wilson, Jesse, and Gina, I'll take £200,000 off the top and give you the rest."

Rory looked totally stunned.

"And since your sister got to keep most of what she won playing poker, this makes you two about even."

Now Rory looked even more astonished.

CHAPTER 14

Getting Crowded in Here

Axel

Occupation: Accountant.

Wanted for: Embezzling.

Questioned regarding missing company funds.

Last seen: Cedar Rapids, IA, USA.

Sydney broke out laughing when she read the next item on The List. "An accountant with a sense of humor; how special is that?" she said to herself.

Axel was an accountant who managed funds for seven companies with common ownership. He collected monthly receipts, paid monthly bills, maintained the surplus in a development and investment fund, and thus oversaw total funds exceeding $17 million. But just after publication of the latest annual report, Axel and the money suddenly vanished.

Alex was gone and had taken all the money with him, or so it seemed.

When investigators checked the resort Axel had listed as his destination, he was registered there. When they called the contact phone number he'd left them, he answered. Then Axel showed up for work the following Tuesday morning as if nothing was amiss. And if that weren't sufficiently puzzling, all the money was back in place by the morning of his return.

Company executives questioned him sternly about the missing money.

"Where did you look for it," Axel calmly asked.

"The company bank account," his supervisor replied. "Certainly, everyone should know that."

"The company has many accounts kept in many different places," Axel patiently explained. "Investments are in various brokerage houses, cash reserves are in several banks, and the bill-paying account is in yet another. Add them all up, and the total will be what it should be."

"But the account balance was zero," the supervisor insisted, "I checked it myself."

"You must have checked the bill-paying account. That was zero because the month's bills were all paid. The balance then remaining was moved to a high-interest savings account. It's common practice.

"Had you talked with company auditors, who prowl through the books every year and question things they consider unusual, they'd have told you the bill-paying account was zero at least three weeks of every month. Money appears in the fourth week from high-interest savings to pay monthly bills."

So, when the huffing and puffing died down, those concerned agreed it had been a huge false alarm, apologized for their steely tone and accusations, and business returned to normal.

And so the matter remained seemingly resolved.

Sydney began to do her usual research by easing her way into the bank's computer system, but an alert suddenly appeared on her screen:

WARNING
You are not welcome here.
Leave now or your computer will die.

An accompanying clock ticked a three-minute countdown.

"I wrote that message," she said to herself. *"My own software is attacking me!"* Apparently, the ever-thorough Alex had obtained a copy of her hack-attack program and had it installed on the bank's computer.

But Sydney had also been thorough. She'd left a secret back door into her program. From memory, she entered a sequence of characters

74

– \$B:L3tm3p@\$\$! – and slipped past the warning. The computer responded:

ALL IS FORGIVEN.
Tread carefully.
I'm watching.

She completed her research without further interruption.

She arranged a lunch appointment two days on with Alex, then drove the 675 miles to Cedar Rapids. When a lovely and attractively dressed woman about his age drove up in a sparkly gold and red Mercedes to pick him up at his place of business, he suddenly got flustered. What was this really about? he wondered. His answer came midway through lunch.

"I was amused by your handling of the confrontation over where all the money went," Sydney said. "You shut down your bosses with an effortless explanation of how responsible accounting and money management can work."

"Thank you," he replied. The axe was about to fall; he just knew it.

"However … you failed to mention one small but significant detail.

The high-interest savings account in question is set up *in your name*, and you personally collect daily interest on several million dollars of bill-paying money three weeks out of every month."

Silence.

"Nobody ever reads bank documents," he finally said hesitantly.

"Tiny print … huge paragraphs … too many pages …" his voice faded.

More silence.

"This could be the end of my career," he said quietly. "I could go to jail." Color had drained from his face. He looked around and was starting to feel trapped.

"I know," he admitted, "I should have thought of that. Have you told anyone?"

"I have not," Sydney said. "I wanted to give you some choices."

"Choices? I can't even run for it. You drove me here in a classy, whatever car that is."

Sydney explained We Remember and the offer of a trip to London.

"Can I leave today?" Alex asked.

"No, but maybe in two days – you have things to settle first. First, draw up new agreements with the bank to put that detail in order. Second, turn in your resignation. Third, figure out how much you would owe if discovered. When those things are done, we can be off to London."

Steven

Occupation: Computer programmer.

Wanted for: Car theft.

Stole hundreds of cars and shipped them overseas.

Last seen: Amarillo, TX, USA.

"Road trip," said Sydney's email to Sandra and Rory. "I need your help in Amarillo."

Sandra walked down the hall to Sydney's office, and Rory joined them by phone from his workshop.

"What's up?" he asked.

"Someone is stealing 50 cars in one city, then 50 in another, and so on. I don't have many details, only that an unusually large number were stolen in Amarillo in two weeks, then it suddenly stopped. The only similarity among the victims is that they habitually parked their cars at the curb in front of their houses. So we're going to Amarillo to interview 50 people or as many as we can find."

"Are we security rent-a-cops this time?" Sandra asked.

"No, just normal investigators driving our own cars," Sydney replied. "We'll each take a third of the interviews. I've prepared a map with red dots showing where each lives and marked which of us should go there."

The map revealed nothing by itself, so they spent the next few days going from red dot to assigned red dot, conducting interviews with anyone they could find at home.

Nobody had seen a thing.

The victims' neighbors hadn't seen or heard anything either.

It was beginning to look like a completely wasted trip when Rory came up with video footage from a doorbell camera. It was dark and shadowy but showed an unmarked grey van pulling up outside. The driver – stocky, maybe 5' 8" tall – opened the van's rear door, extended a ramp, towed the car inside, retracted the ramp, and drove away. It took hardly any time at all.

A separate police report said that neighbors near a warehouse in a different part of town had heard unusual traffic the morning of the last day of the two-week period. Sydney and her assistants drove to the neighborhood and immediately spotted a warehouse big enough to house many cars. They found tire tracks on the floor inside, most from cars but some from heavy trucks. There were also ramp scrape marks on the cement. But the warehouse was empty.

"Looks like they hauled them all away," Sandra said.

Sydney checked warehouse ownership, coming up with All-Ways Freight Lines owned by an endlessly backward proceeding list of organizations, most in foreign countries.

"Nothing there," she said, "at least no one who's going to remember a 5' 8" stocky grey shadow."

A freight dock clerk remembered the delivery of 25 shipping containers tagged as ocean freight with about a dozen destinations. But there were many drivers, none of whom were memorable.

"Let's go home," Sydney said. "I have more research to do."

Setting Snoopers to work, she soon discovered three other instances that came close to fitting the 50-car / two-week pattern: Little Rock, Shreveport, and Fort Worth. The operation was moving west.

To where?

She guessed next would be Albuquerque.

They drove there on Saturday, each with a map showing their section of the city to explore. They would spend the next few days driving residential districts in the early hours, looking for a suspicious grey van.

They came up empty Sunday morning and also Monday and Tuesday. Sydney did remote research on Snoopers and discovered why.

"We're in the wrong city," she told the others. "Car theft rates are normal here, but they're way up in Tucson." They headed south.

At 3:15 AM the next morning, Sandra spotted a grey van in the distance parked in the middle of the street. She idled at the curb and watched as the driver dragged a car up a ramp with a cable, shut the back door, and drove away. She followed.

The truck stopped at a darkened warehouse, waited as the front door rose, then pulled inside. Sandra drove in behind him, her headlights revealing row after row of cars parked inside.

"Found him," she texted Rory and Sydney, "join me here," and she sent them her GPS coordinates.

The driver did not exit the van, so Sandra walked to the front and stood in the headlight beams. She smiled and gave a small wave. The driver rolled his window down.

"You want something?" he asked.

"I just watched you steal the car you have in the back. Do you want to tell me about it?"

"I have no idea what you're talking about."

"Come out here and say that."

"Mom said I should never hit a girl."

"You won't."

The driver exited the van and took a half-hearted swing at her. A moment later, he was flat on the ground with Sandra's knee on his chest.

"I see," he said. "Well, since I'm clearly no longer in charge, what say we put on a pot of coffee?"

"Best to make reservations for four," Sandra said, "My companions are arriving." Rory had just driven into the warehouse, followed soon by Sydney.

"Getting crowded in here," the van driver said.

They went to the warehouse office and made a fresh pot of coffee.

"As near as I can tell," Sydney said, "you've stolen 250 cars in five cities. What are you doing with them? And how are you getting them into your truck without alarms going off?"

"Why should I tell you?"

"I'm just curious. You must be using a computer somehow."

"I am, and it won't hurt to tell you before things get awkward. I'm Steven, by the way, in case it matters to anyone. And yes, I stole all these cars, but they'll be gone before you can do anything about it. Besides, you wanted to know how I did it."

"Yes, we do," Sandra answered, "because what I watched seemed so effortless."

"I have a car with a scanner in the front window," he began. "As I drive residential streets, it takes a picture of each parked vehicle I pass, gets its GPS location, and searches out the car's anti-theft features in a database I built. If it can be opened without an alarm sounding, the program flags it as *Easy*. If it can't be opened but can be moved without sounding an alarm, it's flagged as *Don't Open*. If the program sees that the car was in the same place once before, it's flagged as *Go*."

"You just drive around, and this program does everything for you?" asked Rory.

"It does."

"Sounds like it makes it pretty easy," Sydney said.

"I do 'collecting' most every night. The program prepares a list of five *Go-Easys* not in the same neighborhood, and I drive my van, which has the same program and scanner. It buzzes when I come to a car on the list. I park in the street just ahead of it, set the automatic back door to roll up, and an 18-foot ramp to extend and lock in place. I hook the winch cable to the front, open the car and get in, and steer as the winch pulls the car up the ramp. Automatic devices extend from the sidewalls to secure the vehicle once it's parked inside, and I'm gone in 10 minutes.

"If there aren't enough *Easy* cars and I have to take a *Don't Open*, I park the van at an angle. I put a hydraulic jack under the car, raise the whole front end and put a four-wheel trolley under each front tire, then lower the jack and move it out of the way. The winch pulls the car up the ramp and side rails keep it going in the right direction. I load up the hydraulic jack, press a button to retract the ramp, roll down the door, and drive away. Elapsed time is 15 minutes.

"I park the vehicle in this warehouse, then go for another one. By morning, I have five, sometimes six, fresh vehicles.

"What happens when you get to 50?" Sydney asked.

"I make a phone call, and a truck carrying a shipping container comes. The operator winches two cars into the container, fastens them securely, and takes them away. Then another truck comes, and another, until all 50 cars are gone. One million dollars appears in my bank account the next day, and I pack up and head to another city."

"Where are the cars shipped to?" Sandra asked.

"I have no idea, but I do know they're used for private entertainment like demolition derbies and figure-8 races."

"So you don't take newer cars because of their advanced theft protection," Rory observed, "but it's just as well because they're just going to be destroyed anyway."

"I guess it all works out then," Steven said, "and I've given another 50 people an excuse to buy a new car."

"Before things get 'awkward,' as you said, I'd like to suggest something to you."

And Sydney did.

And Steven was interested.

"My problem right now is I only have 49 cars," he said. "I don't get paid unless I deliver 50."

"Take mine," Sandra said. "I was thinking about getting something less matronly anyway."

CHAPTER 15

A Long and Tedious Path

Hendrik

Occupation: Farmer, artist.

Wanted for: Art forgery.

Suspected of forging 17th-century masterworks and selling

them as authentic.

Last seen: Rotterdam, Netherlands.

Hendrik Bleeker lived on a farm he inherited from three generations of Bleekers before him. The enterprise grew vegetables and flowers in a cluster of greenhouses on land outside Rotterdam. It was managed, tended, and its products sold at market daily by descendants of people who had always worked there.

He took no payment from the farm's operation. Rather, he was a landscape painter with a natural talent and a steady hand. He made his living in the employ of wealthy art collectors and the occasional museum, creating copies of treasured artworks to hang on display so originals could be crated up and locked away in secure storage.

Hendrik made the art world news by discovering an unknown work by Egbert Lievensze van der Poel, a Dutch landscape artist who painted night scenes of cities and villages consumed in flames. Van der Poel was nearby in 1654 when 80,000 pounds of gunpowder exploded at Delft. The scene became a fixation for him upon learning his only son had died in the blast. Van der Poel was a well-known artist of the time, unique in his subject matter but not so thoroughly documented and cataloged as, say, Rembrandt or Van Gogh.

Sydney read the We Remember file marked *Hendrik* which contained magazine articles cautiously revealing the discovery of a possible "lost Egbert van der Poel." A flurry of editorials and commentaries appeared each time another step of authentication was completed, on up to an expert's ultimate proclamation to recognize it as authentic and record it in the van der Poel catalog. The painting brought €4.6 million in a subsequent Sotheby's auction.

But though the painting had been declared genuine, there was lingering suspicion it was forged. Likely, this suspicion caused Hendrik's name to be added to The List. The coincidence of an artist who copies old masters well enough for them to hang in a museum suddenly discovering a valuable painting no one's ever seen before and making €4.6 million on it was just too blatant to pass by.

Or maybe it was just a skill We Remember thought they could use. Whether he was a talented individual or a forger, Sydney was eager to track him down. Contrary to his presence on the "hard to find" list, he wasn't.

She contacted Depot Boijmans Van Beuningen, a museum in Rotterdam where the painting was displayed. The museum listed the discoverer as Hendrik Bleeker at an address that turned out to be a farm east of the city. Sydney flew to Rotterdam and drove to the farm. She wanted to find this Hendrik person and begin the cat-and-mouse game that might tell her what happened.

She wandered among the greenhouses admiring flower plantings and waited to be noticed. Eventually, someone discovered her, learned what she sought, and directed her to the house. She rang the doorbell. Soon, she was sitting in a parlor with Hendrik Bleeker, a tall, thin man with bright, penetrating eyes, exchanging pleasantries and wondering how to begin. He did it for her.

"How can I help you?" he gently asked. "I'm sure you didn't fly 17 or so hours to see my flowers and vegetables."

"I'm curious about the Van der Poel you discovered. I know it's been judged authentic, and I wonder how long that process took."

"Nearly a year, as I recall. Experts looked at it, sophisticated X-ray machinery looked at it, and who knows who else looked at it. I often wondered if I shouldn't have just hung it in the house and let that be the end of it."

"I haven't seen it," Sydney said, "but I'll do so before I leave, though I don't know enough about art to add anything to the discussion. However, I want to ask you this: imagine you did paint it yourself, that you set out to create a passably authentic 17th-century masterwork at the level of Vermeer and his contemporaries. What would be involved in attempting such a thing?"

"That's a long and tedious path," Hendrik replied. "Are you sure you're up for it?"

"I think so."

Hendrik gathered his thoughts and began.

"The painting must be done with materials and paints from the artist's time period. It must be in the correct brushstroke style. It must be aged to appear 300 years old. And it must come with documentation – its provenance – showing where it has been during its supposed lifetime.

"Van der Poel lived from 1621 to 1664. Thus, the type and colors of paint are limited to those in use around 1650. It's also essential to study the painter's style to learn what type and size brushes he would use for various subjects and parts of the scene. A village fire at night, Van der Poel's preferred subject, requires far fewer colors than a court or family scene showing dozens of people in all different styles and colors of garments.

"The painting must pass at least rudimentary scientific tests for forgeries. But because a museum has advanced electronic equipment for such testing doesn't mean they will use it. The equipment is complicated and expensive to use, not to mention to clean, and it often takes months to see results. For a suddenly discovered 'lost Rembrandt,' every scientific test available will be put to work. For a lesser-known artist, probably not.

"That's just the preparation needed. Actual work begins with drawings, many variations on the actual explosion site and Van der Poel's other works. From this come decisions about the painting's actual subject and size. The forger would then acquire the proper canvas and stretcher by visiting a low-end art gallery and buying a painting the desired size by an obscure painter from about the same era. He would scrape that painting off and paint the raw canvas grey or white. He would, of course, carefully check the back for dates or artist signatures and identifying stickers applied when a painting was sold or exhibited in a museum.

"Then he would paint the new masterpiece in a few days or weeks and set about drying it. An oil painting of the 'old masters' era takes nearly a century to dry completely, especially where the brush leaves ridges or lumps of paint. Even after years, the surface is still soft to the touch. But adding Bakelite to the paint, a synthetic plastic made from phenol and formaldehyde and discovered by accident by a master forger, creates a fully hardened artwork once it's baked in an oven."

"This is beyond intriguing," Sydney said, "but I have a feeling it's not done yet."

"Not even close; now it must be aged. I found the Van der Poel painting in an outbuilding where farm tractors are stored. With daily temperatures varying from 0°C -25°C and a chance of rain any day throughout the year, along with humidity changes and oily smokiness from occasionally running tractors, tucked into the rafters would be an excellent place for a painting to age.

"The final segment of this journey is the work's provenance. Most important to that is the paper. The forger would search stationery shops, antique stores, and purveyors of old books to find paper that existed in the 1600s. Blank pages in the back of a book published during the artist's lifetime would always be a good find.

"The objective is to produce complete documentation of the work's ownership and whereabouts at every moment of its existence and present it as a chronological accumulation of journal pages, bills of sale, letters, storage records, and so forth, all in the artist's handwriting or in a type font of the time.

"The problem is, the newly created painting wouldn't have been anywhere.

"The forger would have to make it all up.

"The best way to proceed would be to work out a timeline of possible events, then create documents in an appropriate format based on what could be found in the artist's correspondence, which might be collected in a local library. A suitable history could eventually be invented by creating documents through whatever shaky logic might seem appropriate.

"Once a year or more has gone by, the forged painting is retrieved from its aging place and gently rolled this way and that to crack the paint minutely and give it the desired aged appearance. The forger would then reattach it to its stretcher using the same nails in the same holes, write the work's title on the back, and sign it in the artist's hand."

"So, one or two years later, a 'lost masterwork' has thus come into existence," Sydney said. "What happens next? I'm quite sure you don't just post it on Facebook."

"Not hardly," Hendrik said. "And just showing up at Sotheby's with a painting under one's arm isn't sufficient, either. First, the forger must convince a long-time personal friend art dealer of a painting's authenticity. The dealer must genuinely believe in the work's value and become its champion."

"The discovery of my Van der Poel is a good example. My wife was pregnant. My artist's studio was the only suitable room in the house for the new child. The best place to relocate the studio was to put a second floor on the tractor shed. In doing so, workers found the paintings filthy with grime in the rafters. I cleaned the best one up somewhat, took it to a dealer I've known for 20 years, and the process took over from there."

"And most of a year later, it appeared at auction," Sydney concluded.

"Indeed, and collectors and critics and scholars begin sparring over whether or not it's real," Hendrick said. "So, I hope I've helped answer your questions."

"Thank you so much for your time and wonderful telling of it all. You've answered every question I could have thought of."

The main question, of course, was whether Hendrik had forged it.

He surely had. She could tell by the flashes of pride in his eyes and the obvious satisfaction in his cleverness as he spun the tale.

And she wouldn't tell a single soul. After all, who was she to contradict experts?

CHAPTER 16

Didn't See This Coming

Sydney sat at her desk, apparently doing nothing. She was thinking, pondering, ruminating – just sitting still while thoughts ridiculous and practical alike burst into her mind, floated around for a time, then went their way. The prospect of her 50th birthday looming but four months away seemed to be requiring some progress report, some milestone-counting review of what she'd accomplished in half a century. She was hoping this meaningless accounting of herself, to herself, would soon vanish so she could get on with the day's business.

But what business? The $20 million she'd initially left with Dreyfus Bank in Switzerland, plus the often-spectacular earnings therefrom, plus a few million she'd made selling software, plus tons more from taking candidates to We Remember in London, had upped the total to over $32 million, she'd recently learned.

Fantastic, she thought, please accept this gold star for "living up to your potential," whatever that might be.

Rory and Sandra were doing well too. Sandra had four assistants now, and their workrooms were stuffed with dress mannequins of projects in progress, piles of material yet to be cut, and drawings and paperwork for recently scheduled projects. Fashions You'd Let Your Daughters Wear had been an out-of-the-gate winner, with new clients requesting appointments daily. High-fashion customers were okay with purchasing racy outfits but were more particular about what they permitted teenage daughters to wear.

Rory was an odd-job wizard. He understood whatever she assigned him to do at once and was quickly on the way to figuring out how. He was good at research, at electronics, at interviewing, and at following directions. His preferred work was welding and hammering and grinding in his workshop, but he was equally at home at a keyboard searching for someone gone missing or astray.

But they no longer needed her to create opportunities; they functioned well independently. It was time for her to move on.

In a back-and-forth process, maybe this and maybe that and what about something else, she gradually worked out Step 3 of her plan. When its frazzled ends were ironed out, she called everyone together in C. Monica's office.

"I'm moving to London," she said when the pleasantries tailed off, "and each of you will be substantially affected." Startled and apprehensive looks showed on everyone's face, and no one said a thing.

"First, I'm turning the building we're in over to Sandra. You can occupy whatever space you don't already have, except my office, and reorganize things however you wish. This gives you more than double the space you have now. The three years' free rent I gave you has two years remaining, so there's no need to be concerned about that. I do suggest you update the sign outside to something large that reads Sandra Ellen Griffith, just like big-name designers do. You're on your way to being a big name too."

Sandra's eyes grew suddenly wide.

"I sure didn't see this coming," she said.

"Second, I'm giving Rory my business, Bridgewater Investigations, and the We Remember project. There are 78 names on The List, and we've combined our efforts to deal with 11 of them in the past six months. The remainder should keep you busy for several years. Thus, my office goes to Rory as a work and research space. Since We Remember shouldn't be advertised or publicized here, I suggest you have just a simple sign out front that says RMG representing your metal sculpture work. You don't want to lose track of that."

"What about your computer and Snoopers?" Rory asked.

"I already have something just like it being assembled in London. The computers here stay in the office for you to use. I can also use them remotely if I need to."

"Third," she turned to face C. Monica, "I want to join forces with you and investigate We Remember itself. I've come to believe what you originally suspected – that there's something wrong with that organization. I want to know what it is."

"I'm so pleased to hear that," C. Monica replied. "Even though what you've been doing has benefited individuals involved, I'm still suspicious. It would be good to find out if my distrust has any foundation."

Rory seemed suddenly amused.

"What if your investigation puts We Remember out of business before I finish The List?" he said with a laugh. "Or worse, what if it sends everyone involved to jail?"

"Fortunately, we have a trusted colleague with access to a whole building full of attorneys," Sydney said. "But as a fallback, keep paying rent on your welder's workshop."

"No problem there," Rory said, "I bought it."

"When is this effective?" Sandra asked.

"Now," Sydney said. "Start planning your new layout. Meanwhile, I have a list of things to clear before leaving."

She established phone connection with Hendrik in Rotterdam and acquainted him with the opportunity available through We Remember.

"Why would I want to do that?" he asked. "I have work now and then that pays reasonably well, and I'm not at odds with the law for anything."

"I don't have a suitable answer to that," Sydney replied, "but it might be good to know what kind of job they'd have for you. If nothing else, it's a chance to visit some of your favorite places in London."

"Well, I would enjoy that," he said. "When would you be going?"

"In three days, I think. How about I buy you a ticket, and we'll meet in Heathrow Terminal Four?"

"That sounds just fine."

Next, she contacted Steven. He'd ended his contract with whoever hired him to steal cars and was concerned about repercussions. He was also anxious about possibly being arrested by US authorities for stealing 250 cars and being investigated for not filing state or federal tax returns on the $5 million he'd been paid. We Remember's promise to settle those issues sounded like a good opportunity. He was relieved to learn they'd be going to London in a few days.

Lastly, Sydney prepared an invoice for £655,000, representing the last of her involvement with The List. It would handily cover the new apartment, computers, and anything else she might need in London.

She met again with C. Monica just before departing.

"What exactly is it about We Remember that triggers your suspicion?" she asked.

"They don't operate like a business," C. Monica replied. "They don't exercise any control over what they do or hire other people. There's no evidence of the slightest attempt at planning or budgeting. For example, they turn you loose to hunt down a list of people but provide no direction: not which ones to find first or last, no indication of what or if they'd pay you, no process to follow when someone you locate chooses not to go to London. They're like teenagers with a boxcar full of money, just spending it with gay abandon."

"My concerns are similar," Sydney said. "They don't seem to care what anything costs. I give them an outrageous invoice for about five times what the work is worth, and they pay it. Other nations apparently fund them, and each one throws in 40 or 50 million per year, likely just pocket change to them. They're pleased I'm finding the people they're seeking, so don't stop to question the bill."

"Sounds like you have a rich field of irregularities to sift through, Sydney," C. Monica said. "Keep in contact with me as you proceed so I can help you wherever possible."

Much to his relief, Sydney flew to London with Steven, met Hendrik at Heathrow as arranged, and accompanied them to We Remember. She thought briefly of making an appointment but didn't want to rob the receptionist of her opportunity to harass her about it.

Ms. Goldenrod wasn't pleased to see Steven.

"Part of our arrangement with you is we settle with people you wronged so they don't continue to pursue you. You stole cars from 250 people in five different cities. That means 250 car thefts for us to find out who owned the car, what insurance company they dealt with, and what settlement was reached. You left quite a mess for us to clean up."

"Will this help?" Steven said, pulling a flash drive from his pocket.

"What is it?" Ms. Goldenrod asked.

"There's a file on here giving details of every incident: car make and model, the location from which it was taken, date and time of day, and name and address of the owner of record. There's also a voucher for £400,000 you can print and cash to help with the cost."

"Well, aren't you the thorough one? Thank you very much; you're the only one who has ever offered to help pay for something. I'm hereby declaring you Employee of the Month. I think you will like the job we have for you, by the way."

"What job might that be?"

"Our computer department has a squad of technicians who develop specialized applications like the one you did for stealing cars. You'll fit right in."

Hendrik had no wrongs to right since his "lost Van der Poel" was accepted as genuine by all but a few die-hard skeptics. His job offer in London turned out to be from the British Museum. They were eager to put his skills to work in their vast collection of Old Masters. Flattered to become associated with the prestige of the Museum, he accepted it at once.

Sydney turned in her invoice and met briefly with the Board Chairman.

"I've replaced myself as your seeker of individuals from The List. Your new contact is Rory Michael Griffith, a close friend whose work I'm sure you'll find equally satisfactory. I also gave my final invoice to your receptionist."

"Thanks for all you did for us in such a short time," The Chairman said, "and good luck in whatever project you take on next."

"Thank you, and speaking of the receptionist," Sydney added, "I've advised Rory not to make any appointments either."

Part Four: Something's Up

CHAPTER 17

It Was Puzzling

Sydney had arrived at Heathrow with nothing but her purse and laptop computer. Once finished at We Remember, she took a black cab to her new apartment, a 17th-floor two-bedroom in Islington she'd searched out and leased online. She found the clothes she'd shipped weeks before unpacked into closets and drawers by the building's concierge as she'd arranged.

She also found the year-old Land Rover she'd purchased online had been parked for her in the apartment's garage. Best of all, a duplicate of her office computer was installed and running precisely where she'd directed. She loaded her personal software from a flash drive in her purse and was fully operational in less than a minute.

Her birthday, now three months away, had been nagging at her. As her initial use of the computer, she made reservations to have dinner and attend Don Quixote at the Royal Opera House as a way of doing something perhaps culturally memorable. She was new to London and had no friends to go with her, but she was perfectly content to enjoy the evening alone. All she had to do was remember to go.

She began her investigation the next morning with research into We Remember, reading every article published about the organization since it was formed. It presented itself as a group dedicated to using books, plays, films, documentaries, art, statues, and so on to preserve memories and great moments in the country's thinking and history.

Early articles invited other UK countries to join and participate in this effort. Scotland, Ireland, and Northern Ireland did so, and each new partner was announced with great fanfare.

The operational part of We Remember was structured into four teams of people: 1) a think-tank group that, not unlike London itself, spent much of its time in dense fog studying a situation and eventually bursting dramatically through with a solution; 2) right-brain extroverts dedicated to finding appealing and showy ways of implementing the solution; 3) high-profile buying agents who obtained implementation supplies and equipment needed from whatever source necessary, however bizarre and costly; and 4) actual builders who made the solution happen.

The We Remember group itself provided specialty personnel for operating this multi-group machine, and funding came from each member nation's annual contribution.

She next followed a trail revealing how expenses were paid, looking for a ledger of how much the organization posted against its bank account. She worked her way into the accounting system and generated a report for the year just ended. Individual entries meant little except for those paid to her.

She'd received three payments.

In the report, the amount of each had been doubled. Somewhere between the bill she'd presented to The Chairman and the writing of a check for payment, someone had taken an equal amount for himself, or herself, or someone else. Sydney next hacked into personnel records. There were 89 fulltime individuals and 38 contractors. Both she and Rory were listed as the latter but not by actual name – they'd been given aliases with their real name added seemingly as an afterthought.

So it was for everyone, she soon realized. Everyone employed there worked under a pseudonym. It was just like The List, where names used were mostly aliases. But why, Sydney wondered. The company had no restrictive security levels or assigned clearances; there was no project secrecy she'd been made aware of or to which she'd found reference. Even The Chairman was called The Chairman by everyone. What was Ms. Goldenrod's real name? Was there also a Mr. White, a Mrs. Yellow, and a Sir Pink employed there? It was puzzling.

She sent Snoopers off for a solution and soon found what outwardly passed for an answer. The founder of We Remember wanted the group's focus to be on the issue to be remembered, not on the people who prepared the remembrance. His solution was to have team members work under false names so the preparation would be anonymous to anyone who dug into it. Somewhere along the way, the original intent was lost or abandoned and translated into everyone working under a pseudonym, thus making the whole practice meaningless. But instead of ending it, they fully embraced it and continued to work in that fashion for reasons most everyone had long forgotten.

Entering information for 127 people for her computer to grapple with took Sydney days and days, it turned out. Then she found data from daily appointment calendars to include. More waiting followed as the computer searched for added details, during which time it produced only an occasional beep or ding or cryptic message on a screen.

When that completed, the entire accumulation of data flowed into the Timeline program, where the computer sat like a Komodo dragon digesting a goat and maintained only a blinking message that said, "still working."

She'd considered selling Timeline just like she had the hack-attack software. There might be a market with law enforcement, resulting in another few million in income. But she'd decided against it. Detectives and investigators accustomed to the practice were more likely to continue with what they had rather than learn something new. And they'd want changes. She wouldn't want to be bothered with that.

Sometime during the night, a structure began to appear across the nine-screen display. Actual names were listed alphabetically in a column on the left, static data (alias name, residence address, project assignment, and so forth) appeared in rows to the right, and events associated with the name appeared in time sequence farther right. Projects and events in which more than one individual participated were linked with stair-stepping, color-significant lines.

Sydney stared at screens tightly packed with data. She confirmed that the four-tiered structure she'd read about actually did exist, at least on the computer. Those groups had done projects of historical, political, financial, and cultural significance, as well as some concerning royalty, and individual project group staff ranged from a single person to as many as 12. This all seemed in accord with what she'd discovered.

Until something wasn't.

Among the names listed on the screen were the nine individuals she'd brought to London for interview. No problem with that, but finding Rachel, Jimmy Ray, and Hendrik assigned to something different than their originally assigned job seemed odd.

Sydney wondered what happened to those fanciful military and government assignments Ms. Goldenrod had explained in such detail. Were they just her flights of fancy?

This discrepancy led further. Projects had been active all through the lifespan of the organization, some lasting a few weeks, some a year or even two. About 25 had been marked complete, another three had been abandoned, and six were in progress.

Rachel, Jimmy Ray, and Hendrik had been assigned to a project called Artifact, which had been active for three months. They brought skills relating to jewel theft, counterfeiting, and art forgery. What kind of project, Sydney wondered, had a use for such diverse talents as these?

Six people were now assigned to Artifact, double what it had been. They must have reached some objective and divided into sub-groups, possibly involving a need for the newly added skills. It would be good to find out what was going on.

It would also be good to know where others she'd brought to London had gone and what they were really doing.

Her wall-sized computer display answered part of the question, showing London addresses for them all. She should find them. Sydney printed out the details and set off to see whomever she could.

CHAPTER 18

It's a Long Shot

Sydney drove to an apartment off Parkhill Road in Bexley, fifteen miles east of London. She pressed the doorbell and Rosalind answered, a questioning look on her face.

"I certainly never expected to see you again," she said. "Sydney, isn't it?"

"Correct."

Sydney entered a spacious, well-maintained apartment. Its furniture was designer-coordinated, and windows gave view of a park across the street. She chose a comfortable armchair and accepted an offer of something to drink.

"Last I heard, you were to be disposing of surplus equipment for MI6."

"That's what I'm doing," Rosalind said. "Some people were diverted to a different assignment, but not me. I'm in a room full of others dealing with everything from fountain pens that shoot poison darts to not-quite-invisible-enough camouflage green trucks that carry troops. It's all stuff they don't use anymore, or that's been replaced by something smaller or more functional. Much of it's just junk but the kind of junk they'd rather not have the general public get hold of."

"So why are you there?" Sydney asked.

"They hinted their procedures might not be as efficient as they could be, and any improvements I could suggest would be welcome. Improvements aren't really what's needed. It's like the Dark Ages in there."

"And you have changes in mind?"

"Tons, but everyone's so stuffy and British. I have to be careful how I suggest something."

"Can you tell me anything about this reassignment?"

"I would, but I'm not exactly sure. It involves someone getting out of prison who knows where something is. There's a group assigned to figure out how to get him to tell."

"Surely they have people way more skilled than new hires to do that."

"I said the same thing," said Rosalind. "Apparently, they've tried everything, but he sees them coming every time and clams up. They're supposed to come up with something new and clever no one has thought of before. Sounds like a three-legged horse running the Kentucky Derby to me."

"And six people are working on this?"

"I guess so, but I've heard they meet every few days as a group, but it ends up being a bunch of people just looking at each other or talking about soccer."

"You're right; it's a long shot."

"But they're being generous enough. They're giving me this apartment at no cost, plus $50,000. That'll keep me from going on the run, at least for a while."

Sydney then drove to a house in the north part of Greater London, where Jimmy Ray answered the door.

"Welcome to my tax-free, also rent-free, home," he said.

"I heard about that," Sydney replied.

"It's also beer- and liquor-free at the moment, sorry about that."

"Not a problem, water's good."

"So," said Jimmy Ray, "I gather you've heard I'll no longer be driving government trucks on top-secret missions, whether or not impossible."

"I did hear that. Too bad, it sounded like a cool gig."

"I thought so too, but instead, we have this prisoner being sprung to think about."

"Is there more to tell about that? I just talked with Rosalind, and she didn't know much."

"There's this guy on his last six months of three years in a minimum-security prison for an industrial espionage kind of thing. He supposedly knows the location of some valuable historical artifact. It's not the Rosetta stone, but it's similar, or so the rumor goes."

"And he's not telling where it is."

"Says he doesn't know, never heard of it, had nothing to do with it, why do you keep bothering me about it? Regardless of what he says, we're supposed to get something out of him, even if it's a wild goose chase or two."

"It could be a hoax," Sydney said. "He dreams up this intriguing but unprovable claim. Everybody bites on it and tries to draw him out with money, special favors, or whatever."

"Possibly, but you'd think he'd be using it to get out," Jimmy Ray replied.

"Maybe he doesn't want out. Maybe he's safer inside. Who knows what might be going on?"

"We sure don't."

"But it does explain why We Remember is even involved. It's an artifact. It may be important. It may change the course of history. Or it may be just another rock or whatever. At least you're not Long John Silver following clues to buried treasure."

"I don't know; maybe I am."

Sydney's last stop for the day was Hendrik, whom she found at a café in downtown London.

"Hello," he said, "how did you ever find me? Also, why did you find me? Haven't you disrupted my life enough?"

"I went to where you're living, and the building manager said you spend a lot of time here."

"They have food sort of like I'm used to."

"Was your assignment switched along with a couple of others'?"

"I'm afraid so. It's too bad because they wanted me to copy about 60 paintings recovered from the plundering during World War II. A gallery would then keep the copy and return the original to the owner. I was interested in that."

"Seems very worth doing; I'm so sorry that happened."

"I can still do that job when I have time for it. It's just not my main assignment."

"Any thoughts on the silent prisoner?"

"I think what we're doing is a waste of effort. They've tried offering him large amounts of money. They've put snitches in the prison population to buddy up to him. They've offered to purge his conviction and give him a clean record. Nothing seems to make any difference. He either doesn't answer or says he doesn't know anything."

"Any suggestions you might want to offer?" Sydney asked.

"I do have one," Hendrik said. "Every day, a driver takes whoever wants to go on a drive a few miles away to a fenced-in park with real trees. The prisoners can walk around or sit and enjoy the natural setting.

Most of them are in their late 70s, so there's little chance of them making a break for it.

"A couple of our team were drivers in their previous occupations. Maybe if we put one of them in as the prison bus driver, he could pick up something from conversations."

"That would be Jimmy Ray," Sydney said. "I just talked to him."

"We all work from our apartments unless there's a reason for a group meeting. I'll pass this idea along when I next get a chance."

"Good thinking. Maybe what you're all doing can pay off after all."

Two weeks later, Jimmy Ray suited up as a prison guard and went on a practice run to learn the route from another guard. He then drove it daily, sometimes with four or five passengers, sometimes with none. The passengers talked about nothing in particular, sometimes including the driver. The silent prisoner rode along a couple of times a week. There was plenty of opportunity for a truck to block the road and carry out a simple prison break, but it never happened. It was just a bunch of older gents going for a ride.

Once, as Jimmy Ray approached an intersection, the silent prisoner asked:

"Suppose you could turn here?"

"Sorry, I have to stick to my route. Any particular reason?"

"Not really, it was just for variety."

A week later, he made the same request at the same intersection. It was then that Jimmy Ray made the connection.

The team wasn't looking for *something*; they were looking for *someone*.

CHAPTER 19

Who Are These People?

"Wanted to turn at an intersection? Sounds pretty routine to me, nothing much like a useful clue."

Such was the reply Jimmy Ray got when he reported the incident to the Artifact team.

"It might be helpful, but what can we do with it?" said one of the original team members. "We don't have Penelope Garcia to do FBI super-searching like you see on TV."

But they did.

"I don't work for We Remember," Sydney told Jimmy Ray, "but I'm glad to help you as long as nobody mentions I'm involved. Give me the prisoner's name, and I'll see what I can find."

With that single piece of data – Daniel Murphy – she put Snoopers to work for two solid days. She dug up Daniel's history from childhood to when he was sentenced to country club prison, created lists of his schoolmates and business-world acquaintances, and searched out mailing lists he appeared on. This produced a roster of about a hundred possible friends and a list of his potential interests.

She whittled the friends down to those who had lived within 150 kilometers at any time and developed their lists of interests. Then she cut the list to those who were alive or had been up to five years ago, who shared at least two interests, and who resided in the general direction of a "turn at that intersection."

Six names remained: one who had retired and bought a goat farm, one who sold repossessed properties for a bank, two who had recently died from long-term illnesses, one in an assisted living home, and one who taught English in China. Sydney gave their information to Jimmy Ray, and he, in turn, enlisted the two other team members to go on interviews.

The goat farm owner vaguely remembered Daniel from high school.

The daughter of one of the deceased remembered he'd played cribbage with her dad once a month. None of the other deceased's family recalled the name at all.

The bank repo sales agent said Daniel had bought a property from her, then resold it several months later.

The man in the assisted living home sat watching TV and humming and didn't seem aware of their presence. Others in the room said he was not doing well that day but occasionally had times when he told stories of his past.

By phone, the China English teacher irritably remembered Daniel as someone who had swindled him out of $15,000 and was not eager to see him again.

Jimmy Ray sent the results in an email to Sydney.

"I think you have three possibilities from this list," she wrote back, "the dad who played cribbage, the bank repo lady, and the assisted living guy. Do you have pictures of any of them? I found a few in my searches, but they're only somewhat useful. I would also like pictures you have of Daniel."

It took a week to get a suitable selection of photos. Sydney sorted through them and ended up with a pack of 12 with decent images that she forwarded to Hendrik.

"Go to the assisted living home," she told him. "Choose a wall in the common room where they assemble to watch TV and paint these pictures on it as large as you have space for. If they gather round and ask questions about what you're doing, so much the better. The idea is to make them curious and for our assisted-living guy to recognize himself and perhaps Daniel. I'll write you a letter of authorization in case anyone asks."

Hendrik went to the address Sydney gave him, a facility about 130 kilometers away. Once the front desk person saw his work overalls and what looked to be a tool kit, he waved the artist on through. Nobody greeted him in the common room, so he selected the largest blank wall and started work. He completed one painting in about two hours, another in an hour and a half, and by early afternoon, was finishing about one per hour.

He was attracting an audience. People walked up to where he was working and watched silently. Then one tugged at his shirt.

"Who are these people?" she said with a puzzled expression.

"I don't know," Hendrik replied. "Do you recognize anyone?" She fell silent.

"How do you do that so fast," another wanted to know.

"I do it often and know where things go."

"That one looks like my mom," one said. "She must be famous to get her picture on the wall. I'll have her look at it next time she's here." Others in the group shook their heads. The woman's mother had been dead for 20 years and had never been to visit.

"That looks like *him*," a man said, pointing to the person watching TV and humming. "His name is Frederick."

"Maybe you should tell him," Hendrik said.

"Not today. This isn't a good day for him."

"Maybe he'll find it himself on his next good day."

He finished the last painting in early evening and got ready to leave.

"Who came up with this idea?" said the person who had monitored the group all afternoon.

"I don't know; I just got a pack of pictures in the mail and an order to paint them on the wall."

"They look pretty good. Thanks for making our day more interesting."

"Here's my number," Hendrik said, handing her his card. "If someone starts talking about any of them, call me about what they say."

He called Sydney on his way home.

"It's done," he reported. "They look pretty nice."

"Any reaction from the residents?"

"Nothing useful, but they all were watching and asking questions. Maybe we'll get something more helpful over time."

"Maybe so."

"Thanks for the painting assignment, by the way. It was good to paint a face and a tree and such."

"You're welcome."

"But I was thinking on the way home," Hendrik went on. "Since Daniel is mustering out in the next few months, maybe we should just follow him where he goes, put a beeper on his car or something. If he does know where something is, or where someone is, he'll eventually lead us right to it, or him, or her.

"But later, I thought he was probably in no rush to get whatever this artifact is, so he'd probably just wait us out. Tagging along behind him for a year or so would get old. I wouldn't be keen on that."

CHAPTER 20

She Was an Art Collector

Sydney resumed looking through the Timeline display of employees and contractors. There were clusters representing meetings, sometimes two people, occasionally four or more. Most often, they took place in the We Remember building, but other times at a restaurant, and now and then in a different city. She displayed a list of people who were in meetings most frequently and a list of people – likely vendors – employees met out of town. These were exploratory searches that produced nothing suspicious or significant.

The Chairman met with out-of-town people fairly often; among those, some names appeared frequently. Sydney searched each one and found them to be school chums, business associates, someone selling something, and the occasional random stranger, one being a multi-billionaire from Amsterdam. She'd never done business with We Remember and had no history with The Chairman or any other employee.

But she was an art collector.

What was The Chairman's intent if meetings with her were about Artifact? Was he looking for someone to authenticate it, to value it, to buy it? If he were planning to sell it, he or his company would have to prove ownership.

Problems for another day, Sydney thought. After checking for future meetings, she continued reviewing the computer display.

A long-awaited alert suddenly appeared. TREASURE FOUND, it said.

Nearly two years of dogged worldwide Internet searching had at last resulted in a 14-year-old girl named Lily in Appleton, Wisconsin, finding the photo saying, *"You win a million dollars: love, Sydney."*

Quentin the Quintessential arranged for Lily's appearance on latenight TV, where he handed her a check with great drama. She became an overnight celebrity.

Sydney still had people to contact, so got the location of Angelina, Ruby, and Wilson. She drove south across River Thames to Brixton and found Ruby sitting on her fourth-floor balcony.

"This is a very nice apartment," Sydney said.

"A lot classier than what I'm used to, that's for sure," Ruby answered. "This 'how the other half lives' stuff isn't so bad."

"Did you ever get that bartending job?"

"I did, and I'm up to four nights a week, which is way better than working days. There's sure a lot to learn. Just watching, it seemed like you only had to memorize some stuff, and you'd be ready to go. That's true for the basics or if you're pouring beer, but some fancy cocktails are tricky. And some taste so bad you wonder what the attraction is."

"How are you getting along with the customers?"

"Some are so boring. They sit there for five hours and order the same thing over and over again. Or they're fussy and tell you every step of making the drink in detail. I try to be nice, helpful, and understanding, but I've come close to punching one or two of them out. I don't know if I'll ever be good enough to run a bartending school."

"Sounds like you're learning more than you think."

"I like it a lot. Stop by sometime, and I'll make you a drink."

"I'll do that. Practice up on your martini; very dry."

Wilson declined We Remember's offer and returned to his family in Florida. No matter how much money the new job offered, he'd concluded, the weather was better at home. Maybe he would learn to play golf.

Angelina now lived in Pimlico, not far from the Thames.

"Well, isn't this comfy," Sydney said when Angelina welcomed her in.

"It's pricey for a one-bedroom apartment because the neighborhood is so historic with places like Hyde Park, the London Aquarium, Westminster Palace, the British Museum, and a dozen others. But it works fine for me. It's a great place to go for walks, especially in the fog and rain."

"What do they have you doing? Are you working for Scotland Yard as they promised?"

"I am," Angelina replied. "They gave me a tough time over my background check, but they needed an accountant right away. The job is way more interesting than restaurant accounting, so it works well. It's even super-classified, or so they said, so I can't even talk about it."

"Sounds like you found a great spot. Good for you."

"I'll probably be a probationary employee till I'm 108 years old, but the job is great and only a half-mile from my apartment."

Sydney got a text message from Hendrik that read C! She replied OMW. He wanted to report something confidential, so she drove to the downtown café where she'd first found him. He met her outside, saying he preferred to walk a block to a park instead. Seated on a park bench in an open grassy area, he began:

"I got a call from the common room monitor at the assisted living home. Frederick started reacting to the photo paintings last week. He first just looked at them and walked away. A day or so later, he dragged a chair over, sat for an hour, and studied each one. He seemed puzzled but started sitting there daily, looking at the pictures.

"Yesterday, he pointed at one and said, 'That's me. That's my picture painted on the wall.' Others gathered around him as he kept saying, 'That's me; that's my picture. It's my picture, see, it's my picture.' A couple of those watching seemed pleased he recognized himself and agreed with him. 'It is you. I see you in the picture.'"

"That's great progress," Sydney said.

"There's more," Hendrik said. "Some while later, he pointed at another picture and said: 'Daniel. That's you, Daniel, isn't it? I see you, Daniel. You hide things. You hide things in my house. You think I don't know about them, but I do; you hide things in my house.'"

"Wow," said Sydney, "that surely means Frederick is the one Daniel's looking for. The artifact may be hidden in his house."

"Then we should go look for it," Hendrik said.

"No, we'll need permission from whoever owns the house to enter it. We have plenty of time, so wait a couple weeks before doing anything further. Meanwhile, check with your assisted living source every day to see if Frederick has had anything more to say. And please don't tell anyone I helped you. No one should know."

She had three more people to visit: Rachel, Axel, and Steven. Like the others, each lived in an apartment in a seemingly random section of Greater London.

Axel had a fourth-floor apartment with a balcony in Wembley Park to the west.

"I found out we're all getting these ritzy apartments at no charge because We Remember owns them," he said. "They have about 20 properties located all over London. They bought them as bank foreclosures. But the banks didn't want their property inventory to get out of hand, so were offering them at a bargain price. We could thus bypass landlords wanting to know our employment status, income level, credit history, hat size, cat or dog's names, and the like. I just moved right in here, no questions asked."

"That clears a few things up," Sydney said. "If the properties are sitting empty anyway, it makes sense to put them to use."

"Right," Axel replied.

"I never learned what your original assignment was."

"I didn't have one until Wilson decided to go home. They offered me his job as fleet maintenance scheduler for HM Coastguard."

"I understand some other assignments were switched around. Was anyone upset about it?"

"There was some confusion at first, but getting a free place to live and $50,000 for the inconvenience immediately settled it. They paid back the interest money I took, so I'm free to go back to Iowa without facing charges. But I'm content to stay here. Who knows, it might get interesting."

Steven had a two-bedroom apartment in Bromley to the south.

"Did you accept some particular assignment?" Sydney asked.

"Not yet," Steven replied. "I'll let the dust settle while We Remember works out payment on all the car thefts. It should be easy enough with the information I gave them. I can likely occupy this apartment for a year, tour as much as I want of London and the countryside in the meantime, and see if We Remember comes up with some interesting work for me to do. If not, I'll head back to the USA."

"Give them a chance to find something," Sydney said. "They've been more than generous with you and everyone."

Rachel had a small apartment on the 19th floor of a beautiful stone and glass building in Stratford, northeast of London. Her face turned a bit sour when she saw it was Sydney at the door.

"I was rather taken with the prospect of going to MI6," Rachel said. "Then they turned things around so we could look for some mystery artifact instead."

"I'm sorry if I misled you somehow," Sydney said. "I didn't know about it either."

"It's not your fault, but you're here in my apartment, so you're handy to be grumpy with."

"Be as grumpy as you like, but I came to ask you a question."

"Go ahead."

"If we find this artifact, what are the chances you'll nick it and leave town?"

"Zero," Rachel replied. "Stolen jewelry, like a necklace, can be cut apart into individual stones and fenced easily. If this artifact is significant and becomes a big deal, it would be like stealing Air Force One and trying to sell it."

CHAPTER 21

Located the Artifact

Sydney flew back to Oklahoma City for a meeting with C. Monica. They hadn't talked in two months, and it was a good excuse to seek out warmer weather. Though London was advertised as having a warm, dry climate, it still rained about every other day, a fact that native Londoners accepted as a customary part of life.

"Welcome to clear sky and sunshine," C. Monica said. They were meeting in her office as usual.

"Thank you. We have a lot to talk about, but I don't know how significant it is."

"Then begin."

"I found 11 people from The List, and seven accepted job offers from We Remember. They live rent-free in various parts of London in apartments We Remember owns. Four are working jobs they were promised; three others got reassigned.

"The reassignment concerns Daniel, a minimum-security prisoner who will be released in four months. He supposedly knows the location of a valuable artifact so far unknown to historians or archeologists. The Artifact team is charged with coming up with some way of getting him to spill what he knows. So far, no luck."

C. Monica listened in silence, saving her questions for later.

"I've made no contact with The Chairman, or We Remember, since turning my assignment of The List over to Rory. But, I have kept in touch with the remaining individuals and provided occasional assistance. As a result, we may have located the artifact hidden in the vacated home of Frederick, an assisted living home resident.

"Frederick is a pleasant fellow with a deteriorating memory and is only lucid for short periods. He still owns the home, but assisted living will likely sell it to pay for their services once his existing resources run out. We want to search the house for the artifact before this happens, but need permission to enter from the owner. That may not be easy to obtain because of his mental condition.

"The Chairman of We Remember meets occasionally with people from other countries, one of whom is a multi-billionaire art collector from Amsterdam. I've found no information on these meetings, but it's easy to speculate that he might be trying to sell the artifact to her. The Chairman himself or We Remember may try to purchase Frederick's house solely to obtain it.

"Further, Daniel may claim ownership of the artifact, apparently being the one who found it. That may be complicated by suspension of his rights due to being a convicted felon."

Sydney paused for a time, then continued.

"One more thing is a bit of a curiosity. I discovered the bills I submitted were paid to me in full but were posted to Accounts Payable as double the amount. I have no idea why or where the duplicate amount went, but this possibly answers why they never questioned the outrageous amounts we submitted. The higher, the better, apparently; more money for someone else."

"You have certainly been busy," C. Monica said. "Congratulations on uncovering all you have so far. You say you may know where this artifact is hidden, but you've never seen it."

"Correct," Sydney replied.

"And the We Remember Chairman may have designs on it, but you don't know what they are."

"Also correct."

"And the prisoner being released may have artifact ownership claims possibly clouded by his legal status."

Sydney nodded.

"There are solutions for all of this, I'm sure, but sequence and timing are critical."

"I have a suggestion," Sydney said, "and I must confess, it's most of the reason I came back to the US just for a meeting."

"What is that?"

"If I got you an apartment in London, would you come to help me through this? It might take several months, and I don't want to make a mess of things because of not knowing exactly what to do."

"I absolutely will. Don't be concerned about an apartment; I'll have my travel person find me one, get me the necessary Visa and a car. I realize We Remember would give me this free, but I'd rather not become beholden to them."

Sydney stopped by her former office building to see how Sandra and Rory were doing. She immediately noticed they'd taken her remark about rearranging the offices seriously, and dramatically so. The building's front door opened into a vast showroom featuring spotlighted posters on the wall and mannequins in various poses wearing Sandra's latest creations. Visitors without appointments could walk about the gallery and make an appointment or even order an outfit on the computer facilities.

Visitors with appointments were directed to a many-windowed office to the right. Either Sandra or one of her colleagues would meet with them there. The office behind it had displays of accessories for sale and was also used for measuring clients for their garments. Sandra had taken over the entire upstairs, where she and many assistants cut fabric and assembled outfits to meet client orders.

Sydney's former office was now on the first floor in the left rear corner. Rory was there, sitting at the huge computer display she'd left him.

"Hello," he said, "I heard you walking around and figured you'd find me before long."

"You've made quite a few changes, I see. Is business booming?"

"Sandra Ellen Griffith is the talk of the teenage town. Everyone wants something like so-and-so got, but perhaps with a few changes. Oh, and in aqua, or maybe original cinnamon. She must have two or three appointments a day. Every fashion designer wannabe wants to work for her."

"That's wonderful to hear. How about you? How are you doing?"

"I spend half my time working in my welding shop making home or office display sculptures of desert flora or fantasy cars or whatever, or building grand creature monsters that take up much of a whole front yard.

"The other half I work on The List. I located five more people from it and took them to London. Just like you, I never made an appointment."

"Is We Remember paying you?"

"Yeah, nearly $1.5 million so far, and I have three more about ready to go."

"Manage it wisely," Sydney said. "You never know how long this golden goose will last."

"Are you getting ready to drop the hammer?"

"Nowhere near that yet, but it may be an eventual possibility."

"Then, when that eventuality gets here, I'll try to prepare for it. Thank you, by the way, for the job, the equipment, and this fabulous source of income. Am I supposed to split the money somehow with you?"

"No," Sydney said, "you did the work, you get the cash. Did you move that computer downstairs yourself?" she said, changing the subject.

"I did not," Rory said. "I called the company that originally installed it and showed them where I wanted it. They moved it, installed it, and completely tested it out. They even got stands and tables for working on those FBI computers I use all the time."

"They're called Snoopers, by the way," Sydney said.

"So you said, and I can see why. They know everything. In the middle of this all, I've kept Bridgewater Investigations alive by following up on your PI calls. You could say I've had plenty to do."

Sandra burst through the door just then and gave Sydney a huge hug.

"So good to see you," she said excitedly. "I saw that classy Mercedes outside and knew it must be you."

The chatter between good friends continued for half an hour before Sandra raced out for her next appointment.

CHAPTER 22

Vast and Empty

In gathering rain, C. Monica Stansbury, Hendrik Bleeker, and Sydney Bridgewater sat on a London park bench. With introductions completed and pleasantries briefly indulged, Hendrik recounted progress during Sydney's absence.

"Frederick has been more talkative but hasn't added much to what we know. He asked if we could paint a picture of his deceased wife, Zerilda, on the wall so he could remember her every day. He said he missed her, he wanted her near, and he had to tell her sorry for selling all her clothes. Other residents would like their pictures on the wall as well."

"Selling her clothes?" said Sydney. "What's that about?"

"I wondered too," Hendrik said, "so I asked the common room monitor. According to what Frederick said when he was initially admitted, Zerilda would buy clothes and never wear them. She'd stuff them in a closet with the price tags still attached. This went on for decades. When closets were full, he set up portable wardrobes for her in the attic. She stuffed one after another until full wardrobes filled the entire attic by the time she died. Even the attic stairs were inaccessible because, with the attic full, she'd open the door and throw things up the stairs. Some years after Zerilda passed, he sold the lot to a vintage clothing shop. It took them months to clear it out."

"Maybe the artifact is in the attic, tucked in the rafters or under the floorboards," C. Monica said.

"Very likely," Sydney said. She opened her laptop and linked it to the system in her apartment.

"I'm running my Timeline program for just Frederick and Daniel," she said. She was silent for a while, then looked through the result when it finished. "It looks like they met serving in the National Reserve more than 50 years ago. Frederick bought the house around that time, and the attic became inaccessible maybe 10 or 15 years ago, which leaves plenty of time to hide something there. If Daniel did, it looks like he's been hanging on to this thing for a long time."

"Maybe we should ask him," C. Monica said, "but first, I think we should talk to Frederick."

"And ask him for access to the house?"

"Exactly."

"I think my part is done now," Hendrik said. "I'll be watching for dramatic results coming soon."

"Thanks so much for your assistance," said C. Monica.

It took three days for Frederick to become talkative again. Sydney and C. Monica sat with him in the common room and discussed putting a picture of Zerilda on the wall. He seemed pleased.

"That's so nice," he said. "She can be with me again."

"Do you have a picture we could use?" C. Monica asked.

"I have one here in my room. You could use that. There are more pictures at my house, but I don't remember where that is. Plenty of pictures there. Whole books full of pictures."

"Could you go there with us and look?"

"You'd have to find where it is. I don't remember where it is."

"I think we can find it," Sydney said. "Can you take us inside and help us look?"

"Help you look for pictures. I could do that if they let me."

Sydney talked to the room monitor.

"Yes, he can go with you, but one of our staff must go along."

"What about keys?"

"We have his keys. I'll get them for you."

They found the house about 11 kilometers away. Once inside, Sydney headed upstairs while the others looked for picture albums in drawers and on shelves. Frederick seemed unsure of where he was. He sat in a chair, watched the others for a while, then stared ahead.

The attic was vast and empty. Three bare lightbulbs showed that floorboards were wide and, for the most part, nailed in place, and the peaked roof was insulated roof joists with shingles attached outside. Sydney walked the floor in a regular pattern, looking for boards that might be loose. There were many. She dropped to hands and knees, removed loose boards one at a time, and looked beneath them.

Downstairs, C. Monica and the accompanying staff person had found several albums of vacation pictures. They sat in the living room, slowly leafing through them while Frederick pointed out photos of Zerilda from trips and vacations they'd taken. He wanted to take the albums with him when they left and wondered if there were more.

Sydney was two-thirds along the attic floor when she found a package under a board near the roof's edge. It weighed about 10 pounds and was secured in a taped grocery bag. She didn't want to open it there, so she stuffed it into her shoulder bag and went back downstairs.

Frederick seemed dreamily happy, just paging through albums again and again. They waited, looked around a moment, then locked the front door and walked toward the car. There were three people there, obviously neighbors.

"Hi, Fred, are you coming home?" said one.

"We miss you," said another. "It's so dark and empty on the corner with you gone."

Several people standing on their porches waved as if welcoming Frederick back to the neighborhood.

Frederick clutched his photo albums in his arms and silently smiled and nodded.

"He wanted some things from his house," the staff person said, "so we brought him here to find them."

Sydney and C. Monica parked in an empty lot after returning Frederick and the staff person to the facility.

"Let's open this package before we go a step farther," Sydney said, pulling the taped grocery bag from her shoulder bag.

"Under a floorboard?" C. Monica asked.

"Yes, and there were a lot of loose floorboards."

She ripped the covering away to reveal a smooth-faced rock showing a figure resembling a bird. Below were a dozen lines of text containing intricate shapes and figures, none of which looked familiar. Another carving at the bottom appeared to be a building of some peculiar design.

"This is it," Sydney said, "what now?"

"Take pictures of it, then let's show them to Daniel."

The next morning, they drove to HM Prison Berwyn near Liverpool and asked to see Daniel Murphy. A guard brought him to the interview room half an hour later.

"Somebody new," Daniel said. "Are you going to ask the same questions?"

"About what?" asked C. Monica.

"Oh, maybe the food, or the weather, or if the ping-pong table has been fixed," he replied evasively.

"We happened to be in the neighborhood and thought we'd drop by to show you some pictures."

"Happened to be in the neighborhood," Daniel repeated, "that's good. London is almost 300 kilometers from here. Have a nice drive back." He made a move to signal the guard to return him to his cell.

"Pictures…" Sydney said.

"Pictures of what; show them to me."

C. Monica pulled a folder from her attorney's briefcase and spread out three photos they'd printed.

Daniel's demeanor changed from joking bravado to total silence. It was as if his seventh-grade teacher had caught him with cigarettes. He flipped from one picture to another and back again.

"You found it," he finally said. "Did Frederick give me up?"

"He did not. Frederick no longer lives there; he's in an assisted living home some distance away. His memory of things in his past comes and goes."

"But you found him, and his house, and the loose floorboard in the attic."

"Yes, we did."

"I'd like to know how you did that. Maybe you'll tell me sometime. So now what?"

"Nothing much has changed," C. Monica said. "You get out of here in 90 days or so. The artifact will be undergoing analysis in a museum somewhere. Based on my brief review of UK law, if you believe you can claim ownership, you may still do so. The crime you are here for doesn't suspend that right. That is, of course, if you actually found it and didn't steal it from someone."

"I didn't. I found it poking out of the ground on a scree slope coming down a mountain. So yes, I would make a claim."

"Then I guess we're finished here," said C. Monica.

"Thanks for dropping by," said Daniel. "I'm glad you were in the neighborhood."

"Now we turn it over to We Remember," said C. Monica once back at the car.

"Thus putting all players in motion," Sydney said.

Part Five: Lawyering Up

CHAPTER 23

Reminded Her of Something

Sydney and C. Monica approached the We Remember reception desk the following afternoon.

"Let me guess," said the woman seated there, "you don't have an appointment. Of course, you don't. Your replacement chap didn't have one, either. I passed him through anyway because he's really cute."

"I'll tell him you said so," Sydney said.

"Oh, please do that. Here's my phone number as well." she handed Sydney her business card. "You want to see The Chairman, I suppose."

"Uh-huh."

She rang him on the phone. "Two people to see you, sir ... of course they don't ... ok, right away." She waved them on, and they entered.

"I remember you, Sydney; you've been here a few times before. I'm guessing you are C. Monica, our US Counsel."

"I am."

"What brings you to London this time of year," he continued, offering them seats.

"We've been working with your team investigating the mysterious artifact," C. Monica said. "They've come up with beneficial data over the past few months, and the ever-curious Sydney has been processing it through diverse possibilities of where the artifact might or might not be."

"Well, she's certainly good at finding things. Any luck on this search?"

"I can report to you that these combined efforts have been successful. We've located the artifact. We're here to turn it over to the team."

"Excuse me, you say you've located it?" The Chairman said with some astonishment. "Where did you find it? Where is it now?"

"We found it under the floorboards in the attic of an abandoned house north of London," Sydney said. "It's currently under guard in a safe place. Since the Artifact team has invested their efforts in this project, we suggest they complete the process by shepherding it through its authentication process and then on to establish its historical relevance, if indeed there is any."

"If you would arrange a meeting with the team," said C. Monica, "we'd be glad to have the artifact delivered to you."

"I'm out of London tomorrow; let's do it the following day at 2:00 PM," The Chairman said. "This is a critical development. I'm curious to see what it looks like."

"You won't be disappointed. We'll see you the day after tomorrow," said C. Monica, and they left the building.

"Under guard in a safe place?" she inquired.

"It's in the bag on my shoulder," Sydney replied. "I'm guarding it."

"Should you ever want to become a lawyer, let me know."

Sydney took the artifact to a package delivery service the next morning.

"Please build a sturdy wooden crate," she said, handing it to a clerk, "then secure this item inside, buried in loose packing material like it's something you're shipping to a museum." She handed the clerk a slip of paper bearing We Remember's address. "Deliver it here by two o'clock tomorrow afternoon."

"Yes, ma'am," the clerk replied as if it wouldn't be the slightest problem.

Sydney paid the bill, as she routinely did, in cash from her Oklahoma account. This project in London seemed like what she'd been saving for all these years.

She returned to her computer to search for something else she'd wanted to know, namely, was We Remember connected to subsidiary companies? She was all too familiar with companies that owned other companies, which owned other companies, and so on, generating an organization chart that fanned out like a river delta at its entrance to the sea. How big a tangle was involved here? Did it play some unseen part in whatever might be going on?

By the end of the day, she'd discovered that We Remember owned three subsidiary companies, each with a business certificate and bank account but no actual business premises or employees. Those three companies owned five more, those owned 12 more, and those owned 21 more. Many were shell companies like the first three subsidiaries, but there were 27 legitimate, functioning businesses, including restaurants, car dealers, liquor stores, art dealers and galleries, laundromats, dry cleaners, taxi and limousine services, and even a casino. Each entity had a website showing operating hours and directions to get there and describing (with pictures) the business history, products, and weekly specials.

Sydney stared at the spider-web network of connections diagrammed on her computer screens, fanning out over the UK and across the North Sea to France, Belgium, Germany, Netherlands, Denmark, and Norway.

It reminded her of something.

She and C. Monica made it to the We Remember offices shortly before 2:00 PM and joined the Artifact team in a large conference room. The Chairman was there, and he glanced at them with a slightly puzzled look, clearly saying, "Where is it?"

Sydney gave him a "Be patient" look in return.

They didn't have to wait long. At the receptionist's direction, the package delivery driver wheeled a stout wooden crate into the room on a trolley. It was firmly nailed shut and addressed to We Remember. The driver had a pry bar and handily levered off the top.

"It's all yours," he said, wheeling the empty trolley from the room.

Rachel dug into the contents and removed the rock with its carvings.

"Is this it?" she asked, handing it to The Chairman.

"I presume so," he said. "This must be what we've been hunting all these months. Just looking at it, I have to say it is certainly a curiosity."

Questions came from around the room. Asked to tell how it was found, Sydney related the story of how Daniel gave a clue in the prison bus when he asked to turn at a particular intersection, how acquaintances from his past were found living in that general direction, and how interviews of those individuals led to an abandoned home and the floorboards in the attic.

"How did you figure all that out?" asked Hendrik.

"I have a brilliant and relentlessly nosey computer."

"So, here it is, located at last," said Jimmy Ray. "Are we all out of a job?"

"Far from it," said The Chairman. "Just because we have an exotic tale about how we found this peculiar artifact doesn't mean it's real. It must first be authenticated. It is clearly a rock, but what is this bird-like carving all about, and if these are words or sentences, what are they telling us, and where is this peculiar building? When we know those things, we can involve historians and whoever else might be needed to investigate its origin. No, there's plenty yet to do."

"The British Museum is the best starting point for authentication," volunteered Rachel. "They'll either do the work or find someone who can. I would think they'd want to be part of something so potentially important as this."

"Which means we should nail the lid back on and get it on over there," said Jimmy Ray.

As Sydney and C. Monica left the room, the entire team was busy discussing what each would do next.

"Thank you," The Chairman said as they departed. "I don't know how you knew what to do to solve this matter, but you've done us a great service."

"We should keep an eye on him," C. Monica said later. "If he contacts the art collector in Amsterdam, it will tell us a lot about his intentions."

"You're right about that," Sydney replied. "Tapping his phone would be too risky, not to mention illegal, but I can monitor his email and put a tracking locator on his car to see where he goes."

"Yes, do that right away."

CHAPTER 24

Just an Unproven Theory

Sydney and C. Monica took afternoon tea at Bond St. Tea Rooms near Hyde Park. C. Monica seemed anxious and a bit disturbed about something.

"You came here three months ago to investigate We Remember," she said, "to investigate its business practices and our suspicions about what it is doing. Based on what I've observed in my short time here, you've spent most of your time on this artifact hunt. By doing so, you've saved them months of bumbling around with no real direction and have successfully found the thing, but what have you learned about We Remember?"

"Quite a lot," Sydney replied. "The Chairman paid me to find and bring people from The List to London. As I told you recently in your office, the amounts he posted to the accounting system were double what we charged. A ton of money has gone elsewhere, but I have no documentation of where. I suspect it's taken up residence in his personal bank account to support expensive habits."

"What are those?"

"Typical rich boy things: a country estate with a 30-room mansion and full-time hired workers, a Ferrari and a Rolls, whiskey costing $2,500 a bottle, just to name a few. He's taken up the wealthy English gentleman thing."

"So far, he's not winning my vote."

"Additionally, as I'm sure you observed in this afternoon's meeting, he's quick to take credit for the success of others. He kept saying, 'We did this' and 'We did that,' when he did nothing. He's eager to show success to someone.

"But beyond all the hoopla over the artifact, I have a growing suspicion it's just distraction. There's something else going on that someone doesn't want us to see. The details about the prisoner and what he wouldn't talk about came along at an opportune time, and they took advantage of it. The artifact may or may not be authentic, but I believe The Chairman will claim ownership because We Remember found it. Then he'll try to sell it. Locking it up in the British Museum will slow him down but not stop him."

"So, what do you suspect is going on?" C. Monica asked.

"This is borderline heretical to say, I'm sure, but though I believe We Remember to be a legitimate organization doing what it says it will, I think operating inside is a huge money laundering scheme. It has a network of shell companies, along with many legitimate businesses with high volumes of daily cash transactions. Bogus cash enters somewhere in the network and gets processed daily along with it. I don't know how high in the company involvement goes, but I have a strong feeling it's more than just The Chairman."

"How long have you suspected this?" C. Monica asked.

"Since yesterday, so it's still just an unproven theory."

"How would it launder money?"

"We Remember is funded by annual contributions from sponsoring UK nations," Sydney replied. "Let's say there's another source of money, maybe £500,000 per week in cash of small denominations, a mixture of euros and pounds, that arrives in cardboard boxes at some address. That cash is distributed to the network of businesses, where it's mixed in with daily bank deposits. Thus, £500,000 in drug money, or however it was obtained, disappears into the bank in small amounts every day for a week and is never noticed. Those managing the laundering can retrieve their cash and take payment for their services in clean money from the banks."

"That sounds plausible. Can you put some validity to any of it?"

"Possibly, but I need time on the computer."

"Next question," C. Monica said. "How would The Chairman steal the artifact?"

"Show up at the front door of whatever business or institution is processing it now, show a receipt for having surrendered it for authentication, claim he needs it for an event of some sort, deliver it to a buyer and make the sale, then distribute the proceeds to whomever else is involved. And, most important, never tell anyone."

"Pretty easy, seems to me. What should we do about any of this?"

"I suggest we start by having another chat with Daniel Murphy, the prisoner. We offer to help him find a solicitor to represent his claims of artifact ownership."

"I agree," C. Monica said. "I'll work on that and a few other things over the next few days while you settle into your computer nest and determine whether these allegations you are making are or are not true. And by proof, I mean something solid and preferably obtained legitimately."

Sydney began her quest with the benefit of a whole night's sleep and random dreams about finding the proof she needed. She already knew how illegitimate money could be put into a legitimate bank account, but how could We Remember be involved?

Assuming the cash arrived unsorted and perhaps just tossed into a box, somewhere in the organization there must be a machine to separate it by country, then perhaps further by denomination. Such devices were used by banks, casinos, racetracks, and such and cost up to several thousand dollars.

Did any business in the We Remember network have one?

The answer turned out to be Yes. A review of sales invoices from vendors of such equipment showed a top-of-the-line cash sorter purchased six years before by Hammersmith Haberdashery, a We Remember business west of London.

Assuming cash entered the network there, the counted, sorted, and repackaged money would be distributed to the entire We Remember network, British Pound Sterling to UK businesses, and Euros to those "on the continent" to the east. Thus, a package of cash needed to be prepared weekly for each of the 27 businesses in the network and sent to them by mail.

Where would she find proof of that?

She obtained blueprints for the building housing Hammersmith Haberdashery. The building had an 8,000 ft^2 basement but no indication of what was in it. It was a half-hour drive away, so Sydney fired up her Land Rover and set off.

The first and second floors of the building were devoted entirely to upscale men's clothing, catering to a white silk scarf and black bowler hat clientele. The basement, which had an external entrance down a set of stairs, was fronted by a finely crafted English pub serving local beer and ale by the pint and offering a somber menu of spirit cocktails.

She sat at the bar and ordered a pint. She saw a door at the right behind the bar, likely leading to the remaining basement space, and a sign at the other end of the pub indicating restrooms. She went there after a time and saw another door at the end of the hallway in addition to those to the restrooms.

It was locked.

She picked it and went through.

Inside, she found racks and pallets of stored merchandise for the clothing store and shelves full of whiskey for the pub. Next to the inner wall was a long row of metal beer kegs, each with a tube leading to a bundle thereof that connected to the pub on the other side.

There was a freight elevator for deliveries in the center of the back wall, and to its left was a rectangular room with another locked door.

She picked that lock also and entered the Hammersmith Haberdashery mailroom. She took a thorough set of pictures, especially of a batch of preprinted mailing labels, contents of shelves, and various notices hung on the wall. She touched nothing, though she pushed the open safe door farther open to discover stacks of US currency sorted by denomination and other foreign bills. She pushed the safe door back to where it was, closed and locked the doors she'd opened, and returned to the bar. Her beer was still there.

Unknown to Sydney, her visit was displayed on screens in the Building Security office and recorded on disk by their computer. But there was no guard on duty during the day; Security was only staffed at night.

Sydney related these developments to C. Monica upon her return.

"I see you are still using the brute force approach to get what you need." C. Monica said. "Now we know your suspicions were correct, but none of this can be used in court."

"I did think about that, but I realized this is an organizational matter, and such things seldom go to court. They are resolved internally: someone gets fired, someone else gets promoted."

"True enough. So good going, another job well done for you. I don't think I want to know about what other clandestine skills you may have."

"How did it go with Daniel?"

"He said he appreciated the offer but had representation whom he has already engaged. I checked that gentleman out and engaged him to work with us as well – specifically, to file some form of restraining or replevin order to prohibit anyone from seizing the artifact. It will stay where it is unless we review the reason to move it."

"There you go, being all thorough again," Sydney said.

"Anything new about The Chairman? Has he suddenly made an urgent trip to Amsterdam?"

"No, he hasn't gone much of anywhere, nor has he sent any telling emails. We'll keep watching."

CHAPTER 25

Don't Push It

Sydney analyzed pictures she'd taken in the mailroom. Of most interest was a schedule showing when mailings were done and the cash amount in each package. They were not all the same. Some contained a lot, some much less, the allocation likely based on the size of the business.

Equipment in the room included the cash sorter she'd identified, packaging and postage machines, an ancient calculator with a small crank handle on the side, and a vintage computer with a connected printer. The computer was so old it was probably used just to print mailing labels. Postings of daily cash processed were entered in logbooks rather than automated records.

There was a medium-sized safe, the door of which she'd pushed open and shut, on a table in one corner of the room. Sydney surmised cash would be stored there only for a single mailing. Money shown stacked inside the safe was a puzzle at first, but then she realized it wasn't part of any mailing. These were bills other than pounds or euros that would not be sent out but would be taken periodically to one or more currency exchange kiosks around the city.

The door she'd entered was immediately adjacent to the freight elevator. That was undoubtedly where the cash came in in boxes, then went out the next day, sorted into 27 smaller packages.

Sydney thought about deliveries. She knew the destinations of cash going out, but what about money coming in? Where did it come from?

Then, a further thought: if she wanted another go at the mailroom, could she show up, park in the back like she was making a delivery, and ride the elevator down to the basement? When would someone be inside, working?

There were deliveries during the day – Royal Mail, FedEx, UPS, and trucks bearing orders from vendors – so a warehouseman would be on duty to assist. Cash being laundered would be processed at night, but only once a week.

At night was the time to do it. But she wanted help with planning and execution. Help from an expert.

She phoned Rachel.

They met in Rachel's kitchen. Sydney had prepared a drawing of the basement for reference and had also brought the pictures she'd taken.

"I want to get into this mailroom," she said. "I don't want to take anything. I want more time to look at what's there: logbooks, written procedures, and whatever else. I want to know the story behind what's happening in this room."

"Start by planting cameras both inside and out," Rachel said. "Watch what's going on for several days. If that doesn't give you everything you need, we pick a time and a strategy to go in. You got in once by sheer luck. Don't push it."

"How do I know when to plant the cameras?"

"Do the outside first. That should tell you when to do the rest."

Back at home, Sydney discovered what she should have guessed: the company had an existing building surveillance system inside and out. She eased herself into it and tapped into activity recordings for the previous two weeks. She learned many things.

The pub was busy from noon to midnight six days a week. Last call was at 11:00 PM; workers finished up and departed an hour later.

A warehouseman was in the storage area from 8:00 AM to 6:00 PM and accepted deliveries all day at random times.

The mailroom was busy with mail for the haberdashery from 7:00 AM to 5:00 PM, then completely deserted until midnight. On all weekdays, a lone individual came in at that time and went through cash processing and packaging, much as Sydney had surmised.

The person preparing packages put them into a trolley as he finished, pushed it into the elevator around 7:00 AM, emptied it into his van, and then returned with the trolley. He locked up the mailroom just before the warehouseman arrived for work.

Sydney thought about the many conflicting things she'd just seen.

There was an incoming cash delivery every day, so much more cash was being processed than £500,000 a week. It was more than three times that.

The time to do the job was after 6:00 PM on Saturday to take advantage of entry through the pub.

Though there was a keypad to call the elevator after hours, and its code had stayed the same, doing so would alert Building Security.

But she'd been in the mailroom once before, and they'd been watching then. Were they even paying attention?

She met again with Rachel.

"The cameras turned out to be easy," said Sydney, "they were already there. The system is probably as old as that computer in the mailroom, so it was easy to get into."

"What do we know now?" Rachel asked. Sydney told her.

"Since you came to me with this," Rachel said, "I've been presuming we're doing this together. If I'm wrong, tell me now."

"Together," Sydney said.

"Is that because you thought I had some skills you don't?"

"Yes."

"That's good to know, and with that in mind, I think we should do something other than the black mask, ninja raid. Let's go do some shopping, shall we?" You're buying.

Several hours later, they emerged from downtown London shops with high-end dark blue executive suits, plain white blouses, and black chunky-heeled shoes. They would go first to the pub on Saturday night, let it be known they were officials from the haberdashery's main office, and they were here inspecting the operation. Their review of the two floors of men's upscale fashions had gone exceptionally well, and the classy pub was a brilliant touch, but they wanted to be thorough and see the rest of the building.

On Saturday, that's precisely what they did. The bartender even shut off the alarm and unlocked the hallway door for them. Rachel made a show of inspecting the contents and organization of shelves and examining the stone wall around the building's perimeter (England, being an island, has a high water table, and basements tend to leak). Sydney picked her way into the mailroom and took pictures page-by-page through logbooks, mailing lists, policies and procedures, and whatever else each drawer, shelf, and cabinet had to offer. They exited the way they came in, through the pub, and stopped there for a final drink as they departed. Security guards watched with diminishing interest; the bartender had informed them he'd let the two women in for a thorough home-office inspection.

"I have to say," Rachel observed on their way back to London, "this is the first time I've dressed up in a business suit and heels to pull off a job."

CHAPTER 26

This Was Big Business

The new set of photos kept Sydney busy for several days. She discovered first that there were three logbooks, not just one as she'd initially thought. Three logbooks, three mailing lists, and three sets of packages going out each week explained why the mailroom was busy nearly every night.

She chose a random business name from each list and traced company ownership backward. One led to We Remember as she knew it would. Continued backtracing revealed We Remember to be part of Historic England, the government's statutory advisor on identifying and protecting historic places and other aspects of English heritage.

The remaining two random names led to other similarly organized and structured groups within Historic England.

She'd photographed a list of addresses found folded up in a logbook. Most were businesses in the network, but not all. She recognized the office address of The Chairman at once. Two others pointed to offices within Historic England, but the names weren't familiar.

There were other names with unfamiliar addresses but with 809 phone area codes. Those were numbers in the Caribbean, and calling them to see who answered was definitely a bad idea. But Snoopers would know; they tracked those numbers to Barbados and the Bahamas. She marked them as likely contacts to report cash shipments somehow gone wrong.

She turned to the mailing schedule she'd found near the sorting machine. The three mailings were separate, and names within each list had a corresponding cash amount written in. Many had been crossed through in pencil and a new amount written beside it. Sydney totaled the amounts: one had 27 names and a total weekly distribution amount of around £525,000, the second had 36 names and £800,000, and the third had 14 names and £275,000.

This was big business: A total of £1.6 million (USD 2 million) in illegitimate cash moved into and out of this mailroom every week bound for 77 addresses all over the UK and neighboring countries, then on to banks that weren't unsuspecting or unprepared, but it nonetheless deposited regularly in small enough amounts to pass through their scrutiny.

Next came the procedure manual, a tedious collection of instructions on sorting cash and preparing outgoing packages according to the associated schedules. It got more interesting on the final page, which told what to do if a scheduled cash shipment didn't arrive or packages didn't go out on time. The number given to call was one of the Caribbean numbers she'd just seen.

C. Monica, who had been busy with the artifact, met with Sydney for dinner downtown.

"The order for the artifact's protection I had prepared was served to The British Museum where authentication is being conducted," C. Monica said. "Since then, there have been three attempts to obtain it, one by a courier saying he'd been sent to pick it up, another by a dressed-up executive saying he required it for a meeting with the Prime Minister, and still another by a Bobbie with a warrant who claimed to be an Assistant Commissioner. Much to the dismay of each, they were denied and sent packing with copies of the order."

"It would be gone and sold off by now if you hadn't done that," Sydney replied. "Thank you so much."

"I've also been investigating the alleged potential buyer in Amsterdam. She does have tons of money, and she does collect art. She may be interested in The Chairman and the artifact, but we may be imagining that connection just because he talked with her on the phone. Whether he's ever met with her or not, we don't know. Whether he has any plan to sell it to her, we also don't know. She may be just a bystander with lots of cash."

"I don't know anything about that either. Nothing in his email or daily travels suggests any further contact with her. I was thinking he'd use the artifact to score a big payday, but just how, I haven't a clue."

Sydney related her work with Rachel and their information gathering in the mailroom.

"It was *her* idea to dress up as company executives?"

"Indeed it was."

"Certainly a gentler approach than your last visit there."

"We looked so smart and official," Sydney said. "I very much enjoyed it."

"So, what did you learn in the mailroom?"

"This is a much bigger operation than I thought," Sydney replied, telling C. Monica what she'd discovered.

"I believe you now have enough evidence to make your moneylaundering case," C. Monica replied. "What are you thinking you'll do with it?"

"We have choices," Sydney replied. "We could do nothing, return to the USA, and let it sort itself out. Not my first pick, I admit."

"I agree."

"We could pack everything up and confront The Chairman. He would likely say he knew nothing about it, and within 24 hours, the mailroom would be cleaned out and torn down. All physical evidence would vanish, and we'd have nothing but my pictures, which were illegally obtained.

"Or, and this is my recommendation, we give the evidence to someone further up the management chain."

"Who might that be?" C. Monica asked.

"We Remember is part of Historic England, a non-departmental public body sponsored by the Department for Culture, Media, and Sport. Historic England has a chief executive and an assortment of directors under that, including the Director of Corporate Strategy and Business Improvement. I haven't checked that person out yet, but I think that office might be focused in the right area and acquainted with what We Remember does, yet organizationally far enough removed not to be involved in their schemes. Let us take our case there."

"What do you hope they'll do about it?"

"Ideally, they would conduct their own investigation to verify and expand my evidence, draw their conclusions, then administer the consequences according to their procedures."

"And if 'ideally' doesn't happen," C. Monica observed, "they tell us to mind our own business and go home."

"That's about it," Sydney said.

"When do we do this?"

"I have another task to do; then I'll be ready. Meanwhile, if you would make an appointment with this Corporate Strategy Director person, I'd appreciate it."

CHAPTER 27

That Is Outrageous

They were shown to the Director of Corporate Strategy and Business Improvement office early the following week. He was prepared.

"Ms. Stansbury and Ms. Bridgewater, welcome to Historic England. It's good to have visitors on such a glum day." The weather was indeed gloomy, with heavy overcast and steady rain.

"Thank you," C. Monica replied. "We've been in London and the surrounding countryside a little over two months now, and I must say the weather stretches the patience of even the most optimistic visitor."

"Those who live here feel the same way. Where are you visiting from?"

"Oklahoma City, USA," Sydney said. "But I'm sure if Londoners went *there* for two months, they say something like 'Is it always so hot?' and 'This is miserable; how do you stand it?'"

"I've never been to the US," the Director replied, "but I'll keep that in mind. So, what brings you to see me today?"

"I worked under contract for seven months with an organization of yours called We Remember."

"I'm familiar with it."

"My assignment was to locate people from a list of hard-to-find individuals and bring them to London to interview for a job."

"And one of your skills is finding the hard-to-find?"

"So it would seem. In any case, I found 11 people, nine of whom I brought to London, seven of whom accepted a job. At that point, I turned the assignment over to an associate, who has continued the work with similar success."

"Sounds to me like you were doing very well," said the Director, "why the change?"

C. Monica answered this question.

"I serve as US Counsel to We Remember and hired Sydney. She became concerned about certain practices she observed and brought these concerns to me. We came to London together to do further investigation."

"You have my full attention now," the Director said, "as in, what practices and by whom?"

"The first matter was payment. Sydney quoted what she believed to be an outrageous fee to bring an individual to London. Her purpose in doing so was to assess how too-good-to-be-true this offer was. Her quote, accompanied by an equally outrageous daily expense rate, was accepted and paid without question."

"How outrageous?"

"For finding one person and delivering him or her here: £200,000 plus £2,500 per day expenses."

"I'll have to agree with you there," the Director said, "that is outrageous."

"But it goes on," Sydney said. "When We Remember posted my invoices, they doubled the amount for each one I turned in. Whoever pays the bills here is getting way overcharged, and a lot of money is going to some unknown destination."

"I guess what I'm wondering right now is why you would even tell me about this. You had a job that substantially overpaid you for doing something you knew how to do and successfully did, all as agreed. Why would you mess that up?"

"You're in charge of Business Improvement," C. Monica said. "This isn't good business."

"I certainly agree. What are you hoping I'll do about it?"

"That's getting a bit ahead of things, I'm afraid," Sydney said, "there's something much more serious going on." The Director looked at her with guarded interest, clearly wondering what other bad news she'd brought. Sydney continued.

"We have reason to believe We Remember and two of your other departments are operating a sizeable money-laundering operation. Approximately £2.4 million per week is coming in from the Caribbean and being laundered through a network of small businesses connected to your operation all over the UK and, as you say, 'on the continent.' This has been going on for many years."

The Director was quiet for a long while, got up to look out his office window, then sat down again.

"You should definitely tell me about this."

"It started with a men's clothing store in Hammersmith, indirectly owned by We Remember," Sydney replied. "I went there and, in its basement, discovered a mailroom with equipment to process large amounts of cash, written procedures on how to do it, the names of every small business receiving cash and the amount thereof, and a list of contact names including those of three department heads who work here. I've also watched security recordings of the operation, which takes place, fittingly, in the dead of night."

"Whatever prompted you to go there?" asked the bewildered Director.

"They purchased an expensive and highly sophisticated cash sorting machine some years ago. They were part of an expansive business network I'd identified as connected to We Remember, so I wanted to see what they were doing. It was a far bigger operation than I'd thought."

"Where does money go to be laundered?"

"It starts as a large income amount to a known illegitimate source, like a drug dealer or human trafficker." C. Monica answered. "It's distributed then to smaller businesses, like a restaurant or a nail salon, which has many daily transactions. There, it's mixed in with regular receipts, deposited in the bank, and becomes clean money."

"If I'm following you correctly, these networks you discovered are all small businesses owned by other businesses, which are ultimately owned by We Remember," said the Director.

"Exactly, and somewhere near the end of the line, other transactions come along to move clean money from all these banks back to the source."

"This has been extremely educational," the Director said, "but I think we're now back at the point I mentioned earlier of what's to be done about it."

"We can give you evidence we've gathered," Sydney said, "but that won't be sufficient. It would be best if you went where I've gone and gathered your own. Quietly, I might add, so it doesn't all disappear. Use it to build a case that satisfies you, then determine what consequences you are prepared to hand out. Just remember, £2.4 million a week is a big operation. When you shut it down, someone will be really upset."

The Director stood, signaling the meeting was over.

"I don't know if I should thank you, but knowing what's going on is good for me. Thank you for doing that, and thank you for bringing these matters to me. I can't promise to keep you regularly informed, but you'll see the results of any action taken or not taken."

Sydney handed him a flash drive containing the evidence she'd prepared, and then she and C. Monica left the office.

"What do you think?" Sydney asked back in the car. "Is he part of this scheme?"

"No, he is not. The look in his eyes matched what he was saying the whole time. I believe he will do something. What was that final task you had to do, if I may ask?"

"To prepare the file of evidence for him," Sydney replied. "Business people want short summaries, not stacks of data. I organized excerpts from my evidence, showing a few pages from a logbook, then a page of procedures, followed by the phone list with The Chaiman's number and the Caribbean numbers. Then came a mailing list sample showing cash allocations to network businesses, a shot of the We Remember network from my computer, and pictures of mailroom equipment. The full detail came last to bolster accusations we made.

"It wasn't a formal presentation with theatrical graphics, but it told the story."

"Let's hope it does."

CHAPTER 28

Battle Lines Are Drawn

Daniel Murphy emerged from HM Prison Berwyn precisely on schedule. His solicitor arrived just as promptly to pick him up.

"Welcome back to the world," he said in greeting.

"And the world is still here," Daniel replied. "Apparently, I haven't even been missed."

"Possibly not, but several things are on hold awaiting you."

"Like my life?"

"Your life is eager to continue after this interruption for alleged misdeeds."

"Another on-hold example, please."

"The British Museum has your artifact but has yet to issue an opinion on its authenticity," said the solicitor. "At the urging of USA attorney Stansbury – one of the women who visited you – I prepared an order that it is to remain at the museum unless she or I authorize its movement somewhere else, like to a different site to do further testing."

"Sounds like a good precautionary step," Daniel said.

"It was. On three occasions since then, someone has tried to make off with it on one pretext or another. But the museum held fast, and the artifact is still there."

"Brilliant."

"I think it's now time for you to proclaim your ownership officially."

"Have the necessary transactions been completed?"

"Indeed, they have. With your final signature, it will be done."

"Then let us go forth and proclaim," Daniel said.

C. Monica was at the British Museum inquiring about the status of the ongoing artifact authentication.

"We're a long way from finished," the authenticator said, "but we have established several things.

"Clearly, it's a rock; we know that for sure. The bird-shaped figure carved into it suggests Egyptian origin, but the symbols don't match any Egyptian language or that of any nearby civilization. There's a possibility it may be European, possibly even originating with early British settlers. It may be significant to British culture, but we haven't determined that yet."

"How long will you continue working on it?" C. Monica asked.

"Another month or two, perhaps, unless some discovery leads us down a new path."

Many days of waiting followed, during which Daniel began resuming life before prison, and Sydney and C. Monica shopped, ate at fancy restaurants, and went to plays and operas. It was a pleasant interlude but ended abruptly when We Remember filed a court order claiming artifact ownership.

C. Monica was immediately notified and passed the news along to Sydney.

"Daniel Murphy has done so, too," she added.

"So, battle lines are drawn, or at least penciled in," Sydney replied. "Two entities are claiming ownership of the same thing, which may or may not have any value."

Solicitors from We Remember and Daniel Murphy sent letters back and forth, each fluffing up their feathers to insist their case for ownership was valid. They ultimately agreed to request a court hearing and were granted one a week later. Both appeared. The judge listened to their arguments, ordered them to conduct mediation, and set a final appearance date a month later.

Mediation was excellent for conflict resolution. It consisted of each party occupying a separate room and an experienced, impartial individual going back and forth between them to negotiate a settlement. They could have a joint opening session to establish ground rules and enumerate issues in dispute. They did so, then retired to their rooms.

The mediator met with We Remember first, then joined C. Monica, Sydney, Daniel, and his solicitor.

"We Remember is claiming ownership of the artifact because they say they found it," the mediator began. "At great expense, they conducted an exhaustive, months-long search throughout the UK, which ultimately resulted in its discovery."

"I knew where it was the whole time," Daniel replied.

"And when you wouldn't reveal that location," said Sydney, "I followed up on casual comments you made, found it, and turned it over to the We Remember team. They may have possession, but their claim of ownership is a stretch."

"They say further," the mediator went on, "that your felony conviction for corporate espionage nullifies your right to claim ownership."

"Upon a felony conviction," Daniel's solicitor patiently replied, "a person surrenders his or her driver's license, the right to vote and hold public office while in prison, and the right to work with children if the offense is of that nature. There is no loss of the right to own property. My client is no longer in prison, can reapply for a driver's license, and his felony had nothing to do with children."

The mediator left and returned half an hour later.

"We Remember has modified its stance," he said. "They agree with your interpretation of rights surrendered or not surrendered but now maintain the artifact is property of the landowner. Most property in the UK is owned by someone, often back many generations. If you found the artifact coming off a mountain as you claim, the artifact belongs to whoever owns the mountain."

"I own the mountain," Daniel said. "If you can own a cottage in the countryside, I can own a mountain."

"Do you have title and deed?"

Daniel's solicitor pushed a folder of paperwork across the table. These were the "final necessary transactions" Daniel had asked about.

"Looks like you do," the mediator said. "I must say your opponent's case for ownership is getting weaker by the minute. You should probably be prepared to give them something."

"They can bid on the artifact if it goes to auction," Daniel said.

Mediation ended there. They now had to wait a month for the final appearance before the judge.

Sydney contemplated moving back to Oklahoma City. She'd been in London for seven months but wasn't particularly attached to it or Oklahoma. It took roots to be attached. Though she'd lived in an apartment in both places, an apartment wasn't roots. Family was roots, but she had none of that either. Sandra and Rory might be considered family, but Sydney didn't want to be like the lonely maiden aunt who hangs around someone's life, giving the idea she was expecting something.

This might be another crossroad, she thought. The previous such occasion, after visiting Quentin the Quinessential's office nearly four years before, had worked out very well. Maybe, if she thought it through properly, this one would too.

CHAPTER 29

Bring These Guys In

A week before the final court hearing on ownership of the artifact, Sydney learned police had raided the Hammersmith Haberdashery mailroom at three in the morning and confiscated every scrap of paper, every stack of currency, and all machinery and equipment. They arrested the operator on duty and locked and sealed the room.

When The Chairman and the two other involved department heads arrived at work later that morning, police arrested them and took them to headquarters. There was much talk of "There must be some misunderstanding" and many wide-eyed looks from people poking their heads out of office doors and cubicles, but the officers were quite firm with their orders to "bring these guys in."

Sydney realized at once her work had ended. The day belonged to the Director of Corporate Strategy and Business Improvement now; she should stay far away unless called. He had her evidence. He'd obviously verified it with the actual documents. She had no part in it now.

C. Monica had returned to Oklahoma City three weeks before. She'd found all to be in order: her attorneys were still busy in thei offices, her desk was not stacked with unopened mail, and a new vase of fresh daffodils stood on the credenza. Five months in London had been exciting, and working closely with Sydney again was a joy. It had been one of the few times she'd done work outside her office, and it had been a pleasant experience. But this was where she belonged. She was glad to be back.

She took Sydney's call regarding the raid and the arrests. It was good to know their efforts had amounted to something, and consequences might be levied on a few who broke the law. But it seemed far away now and long ago.

Rory received notice that The List had been withdrawn, and he was out of a job. But We Remember, under a new department head, made a generous offer to consider his work in progress. He'd be paid the customary full amount if he brought the latest individuals to London.

He did so, collected £600,000 plus expenses, then returned and invited his sister to lunch. But not just any lunch. He chartered a jet to Charleston, South Carolina, and they had crab cakes and high-end bourbon at 82 Queen.

He told his sister that though his job had disappeared, he was still fully busy welding metal art and doing Private Investigator work for Bridgewater Investigations.

Sandra reported she'd been invited to present as fashion designer Sandra Ellen Griffith at New York Fashion Week alongside the most famous of the famous designers. She'd gone there and presented a dozen of her recent designs. The audience, apparently disappointed that she offered practical designs that ordinary people would wear and none were naked dresses with filmy, transparent fabric, gave her weak, unenthusiastic applause and rated her work as schoolmarmish. Afterward, however, she received $300,000 worth of orders, which she took as the kind of mixed message she'd welcome anytime.

The final court session on the artifact proved anticlimactic. Sydney, Daniel, and his solicitor attended, but only the solicitor for We Remember appeared. He allowed that since their case had fallen apart, getting The Chairman out of jail for an afternoon wasn't worth the trouble.

The judge ruled in favor of Daniel and declared the artifact to be unquestionably his. He ultimately sold it at a Sotheby's auction to a collector phoning in Liverpool. The collector immediately loaned it to the British Museum for display. Daniel used the $2 million proceeds to build a house on the mountain he owned.

The money-laundering case labored on for a month, primarily due to elaborate maneuverings of solicitors and Crown prosecutors. Nobody represented the hapless mailroom operator who maintained "he was just doing a job." On the day of sentencing, he received a stern lecture from the judge for "just standing by and not reporting," along with three years in jail.

Though The Chairman and his two compatriots and their table full of solicitors maintained they "never knew what the money was from" and were "just carrying on a procedure already in place," the judge was unsympathetic. Considering they'd overseen laundering of nearly £500 million in six years, he sentenced them to the maximum of 14 years.

There came then a discussion of Witness Protection. Police had confiscated nearly £3 million in the raid, and the owners of that cash were not known for being forgiving. Solicitors pleaded that their clients were in danger of retribution from these individuals.

The judge dismissed this summarily, saying, "Witness Protection is for witnesses; your clients are the perpetrators." In other words: "You shoulda thought about that."

Thus, the money launderers went to jail, the evidence was packed into boxes and sent to storage, and the Hammersmith Haberdashery mailroom was unsealed, torn down, and repainted. The resulting space became part of the storeroom. Since most of the 77 participating businesses were out of UK jurisdiction, they received only a summary of the trial and an explanation of their role in the crime committed.

The Artifact team was dissolved, and its members, including Rachel, Hendrik, and Jimmy Ray, scattered like dandelion fluff in the wind, going off to their initially assigned jobs. At last report, they were all doing well.

But a particular group in the Caribbean noticed their incoming flow of money had stopped, and nearly £3 million had disappeared. They wanted it back.

A short time later, two surly men in ill-fitting suits and sand-colored fedoras, one tall and slim, the other short and plump such that they looked like the number 10 walking down the street, landed in London and went to Hammersmith Haberdashery. They demanded to see the mailroom. After much threatening and disturbance of customers at the bar, they were taken there. The mailroom was gone. The bartender told them it had been torn out weeks before.

They had the name of the mailroom operator and went to his home. He wasn't there. He was in prison.

They had the names of the three department managers who'd participated in their money-laundering scheme, so they went to Historic England's offices. They learned those individuals were in prison as well. They were also told that none of the money they considered theirs had ever passed through the premises, so it wouldn't be found there either. Historic England bore no responsibility for "their money." Pressing their demand further with outright threats of violence would result in quick attention from building Security and the law.

They also had the names and locations of the 77 businesses that had unwittingly cooperated with the scheme. They traveled to a few larger ones but quickly discerned they'd find nothing there. The money had come in. The money had gone out. Demanding and threatening and shooting people wouldn't bring it back.

They didn't know about Sydney or Rachel and the low-profile but effective part the two had played in their scheme's undoing. So, the two surly men in ill-fitting suits and sand-colored fedoras boarded a plane and flew back to the Caribbean. There is no record of what happened to them there.

A similarly surly individual snooped around Tucson looking for Steven, who had, in the group's estimation, welched on a contract. Steven wasn't there. The similarly surly individual then went to Amarillo. Not there either. He found the same in Fort Worth, Shreveport, and Little Rock. Steven had skipped, he figured, and he also took a plane back to from wherever he came.

In truth, Steven was doing fine and gainfully employed in London. Another gentleman from the Caribbean, who looked and dressed like Harry Belafonte singing about bananas but could be as nasty as a cornered wolverine, *did* know about Sydney and C. Monica. He traveled to London to look for them. Neither was there. He went to We Remember and Historic England but was rebuffed like the others.

He then went to Oklahoma City. He found no trace of Sydney Bridgewater but did find C. Monica Stansbury. He burst into her office unannounced and fiercely demanded she pay him the missing £3 million, or USD 3,814,725.

She gave him The Stare. That piercing, unsympathetic, repent-now stare like your mother's when you'd done something shameful.

He withered before it. He fell silent under her pitiless gaze.

"Get out of my office," she said sternly. "Make an appointment."

He fled, and like others before him, boarded a plane and returned empty-handed.

CHAPTER 30

One Step Ahead

Meanwhile, like her hero, Xander Moorhouse, Sydney was still one step ahead.

She'd checked Step 3 off her plan.

Her goal of aiding herself, a friend, and someone not her friend had been achieved.

This brought her to a familiar crossroads. But this time, any path forward would work. She had no particular journey's end so one way was as good as any other. It was a case of "If you have no destination, you can never be lost." Thus, with no farewells of any kind, she just disappeared.

She wouldn't be found in London.

She wouldn't be found in Oklahoma City.

Research would show she'd bought out the lease on her London apartment, given away her Land Rover, and had her clothes – including the $40,000 worth of high-fashion shoes and dresses – and all her London computer components shipped to Oklahoma storage.

Research would also show she'd vacated her Oklahoma apartment long before but had come to town long enough to reclaim her Mercedes Maybach and drive away.

What research wouldn't show was any trace of Sydney.

The last person to see her was Ruby, who, in the London pub where she tended bar, made Sydney a Bombay Sapphire martini, with but a (whisper) of vermouth, stirred, not shaken.

Tahiti was the first stop after her disappearance – because sipping a martini in late afternoon, and another watching sunset, suddenly seemed like *such* a good idea. She would try that out, if only for a few days. Then she would go … somewhere … and had plenty of time to decide where.

C. Monica Stansbury's phone rang a year later.

"I've been looking for Sydney Bridgewater, and I understand she worked for you some time ago," said an unfamiliar voice.

"She did."

"I'd like to find her and offer her a job. Her skills seem almost legendary, according to what I've heard. I believe she's just what I need for my business. Do you happen to know where she might be?"

"No, I do not," C. Monica replied. "I'm afraid you'll have to keep looking."

"That's what I've been doing but without any luck."

"I can tell you one thing for certain."

"What's that?" the voice said eagerly.

"Don't look in North Dakota."

– THE END –